NEW WRITING
VOLUME 3
SPRING 2025

SERPENT CLUB PRESS

SCP

Printed in the United States of America
Set in Williams Caslon
Designed by Emily Gasda

ISBN
9798985267648

Cover art by Jennifer May Reiland
Detail from "The Banner of the Five Wounds"
15 x 24 in / Gouache on Wood / 2023

NEW WRITING
VOLUME 3
SPRING 2025

Edited by
Matthew Gasda and Paul Franz

TABLE OF CONTENTS

Vengeance

Ross Barkan

In the new century, Tad came back. Enough time had passed in the shadowed rib of the strange country.

What he wanted to do, really, was change his name, and if his life had been lived by the laws of cinema or novel-making, he would have done it immediately. But there were ordinary bureaucratic impediments he didn't want to meet head-on or encounter at all. Paperwork to submit, documents to verify, slow-building confrontations in dimly-lit offices.

He would remain Tad Plotz. He could always say his name like a curse word.

In the new year, he got a job delivering Chinese food, riding a bicycle through the deranged street grid of Queens. His mother and father didn't know he had come back to New York. They didn't know much of anything.

He had last sent a letter to his sister at the end of 1999, wishing her a happy millennium. That was over a year ago now. Maybe he would send another. Maybe he would finally change his name.

He took a two-room walk-up in Jackson Heights, confronting the elevated train. For years, he had retreated from noise, seeking out the desolate towns along interstates, wading through weed-strewn lots to get his groceries. He had enclosed himself in rural Michigan, stared down death along the lake. He had systematically made the attempt to excise his past so he was merely a free-floating being of the present day, without memory and beyond time, but he would, despite his painful efforts, crumble inward, into himself.

Past thirty now, he needed to figure out what to do.

New York City was inevitable. It was the nightmare at the edge of his consciousness, its logic brute and unrelenting. A city was easier to disappear into than a forest. He delivered on the late shift, reporting to Wilbur Chiu, who owned the restaurant, Blue Star. Chiu was a serious man and he seemed to understand the New York nightmare very well. He spoke to Tad, at first, in clipped, single sentences, his eyes dark and shimmering behind rimless frames. Chiu usually worked the cash register, dismissing his subordinates to the kitchen, where they could cook or watch others cook. He seemed to welcome the unspoken collisions of the everyday, the stoners hunting glasseyed for spring rolls, the working mothers scrounging up pork fried rice for their children, the cab drivers guzzling cans of Coke between shifts. When he crossed his arms and stared, his eyes and lips would freeze as if he were receding in time, taking on the glory of a Romanesque icon. Tad was sure that Chiu, who hardly spoke to anyone and seemed to dwell alone, had once lived in ways that were unfathomable.

"Don't fuck this up," Chiu told him.

It had been years since Tad rode a bicycle but he took to it easily. He knew how to pedal and pedaled. Soon, he was good enough to slash his way between trucks and taxi cabs, challenging motor vehicles for his parallel seam of asphalt. Every few minutes he heard the machine pulse of the overhead subway and tried to hear the people inside, the thousands in communion with their work. He could pedal for Chiu forever, he decided. There were soldiers who died for generals. They collapsed in their own blood for ideas bigger than themselves.

When he wasn't working, he had time. Less than he used to when he lived in the cabin in Michigan's outer reach, but enough to create a certain pressure to fill it. That was the city. He was reacclimating himself. What he knew was that he had lost weight, too much, and his hair was long, too long, and he made a concession to vanity by going to the barber and buying dumbbells at the local sporting goods store. He would be a better version of himself for no one.

His apartment was spare, bereft of paintings, photographs, bookshelves, and dishes. He bought paper plates, plastic silverware, and positioned a single table in the middle of an empty living room with a pair of windows aimed at the elevated train tracks. When he walked the wooden floorboards, he heard a creaking that seemed too loud for his body, as if someone from below were threatening to break through. The walls were plaster, thin to the touch, and he sometimes dreamed at night the apartment would crumble, burying him in paint chips and ash. Next door, a husband and wife shouted about a baby. Their fights, peaking at five p.m., took on a rhythm he began to anticipate, and without a TV, a radio, or a computer, he found these intermittent clashes worth the struggle of staying awake. At seven, he began delivering for Chiu, finishing in the early morning. There were times Chiu was awake to greet him when he returned, his thick arms folded in front of the cash register.

One Saturday in the spring, when the ice had thawed and the back of his neck was warm with sunlight, he pedaled to the Central Queens Library in Jamaica. He would never buy a book but he could read them for free. Chiu had him delivering six days a week, which he preferred, and he decided to use some of the free hours to discover what his brain could still process. In his hoodie and dark jeans, he almost looked like everyone else, another man dimly on the move.

He read books about crime. Studies on murder rates and recidivism, how prisons were built, the unionization of police. In this section, the world was a series of cages to escape into or from, all nations evolving together in an effort to contain the worst impulses of the human species. The only crime he had committed, as far as he knew, was using drugs. All behavior, in the right circumstance, could be a crime, with the proper confluence of power and paranoia. He sat on a small wooden bench and read for hours, shadows creeping over him.

He ate more. His bones no longer announced themselves on his veined skin. He had flesh, light muscle and fat, and his skin took on new color, a tan from walking and biking in the sun, a blood flow to make himself less pallid. He had always been drawn to routines and now he had another: Saturdays would be for the library.

He passed whole weeks speaking to no one but Chiu. Even when he delivered the food, he nodded politely and extended the brown paper bag, the heat of the meat warming his palms.

There were times he considered his family. He had no friends anymore. But there was no way of undoing the reality of having been a child born to two parents, having been the older brother to a younger sister. They were all still out there somewhere, his own existence an offshoot of their own.

Delivering food at night meant seeing a city few wanted to see. If in daylight the city seethed, at night it seemed to exhale, like a sibilating beast bringing itself to heel. He passed vacant blocks lit only by neon, hookers roaming the pavement, lone men in caps smoking against brick walls. The homeless came in small, roving groups, pushing shopping carts, huddling in swollen jackets of professional football teams, staring Sphinx-like from their chosen street corners.

Twice, he was mugged. The first time was typical but almost deadly, a man with bloodshot eyes and a bent knife thrust straight out, an announcement of rage. He was older, a thick beard curling off his cheeks.

Gimme everything you have, he said. Gimme everything you have.

Tad complied. The cash amounted to forty-six dollars and twelve cents. He was in the middle of a delivery and the man demanded the food too. Gimme everything. This bothered him more. The large order of sweet and sour chicken with pork dumplings and fried rice (free can of Coke) was not his. Whomever he was delivering it to was hungering, in the early morning, for a meal and now it would not come. Chiu wouldn't be pleased. It was his reputation on the line.

Gimme all of it.

The man with the bent knife took the plastic bag of Chinese food and dashed in the opposite direction, determined to disappear. Tad would never see him again.

The second time, three months later, the mugger was younger, eighteen at best, and he held a gun straight at Tad's temple.

"C'mon," Tad begged. It was two o'clock in the morning.

"Turn it over, now."

This time, the mugger got fifty-one dollars and fifty-eight cents. To Tad's surprise, the barrel of the gun touched his skull. It was only brief, a fleeting moment of connection, and the fear he felt was deeper and stranger than any he had known. He could have died from it alone. He could tell the mugger didn't want to shoot, that he regarded the gun as a prop. But his lack of intention made Tad fear that dark luck would dispatch the bullet from the chamber anyway and bury it thoroughly in his brain. He was a kid who seemed to make mistakes. As Tad watched him scrutinize the dollar bills in his small hands, he saw how slight he was, nearly shaking.

"Leave the food, at least," Tad said.

"I don't want your fucking stinky ass Chinese food."

Even the way he spoke wasn't entirely convincing. The robbery was for someone else. He could almost feel sorry for the kid because the kid wasn't going to take a real cut from it. The cash would be divided and redistributed up the food chain, away from him. He was a prole mugger, performing grunt work for another. Somewhere, in a house with central air-conditioning, someone would count the money the kid rightfully stole. It was true: Chinese food meant nothing in this marketplace. Even Chiu's.

The kid, for good measure, pointed the gun one more time. The cash had been safely stashed in a side pocket. He held the gun for another moment, backpedaling into the darkness.

"See you later," Tad said when he was gone.

He resolved never to die on these streets, delivering for Chiu. When he returned to Blue Star, Chiu was hunched over the counter, reading one of the Chinese papers printed out of Flushing.

"No delivery?" Chiu asked. "Robbed again?"

"A kid with a gun got me."

"It was worse ten years ago. He would have killed you."

"What made ten years ago so special?"

"With more killing, more could be killed. It meant less to lose an individual."

"I'm going to go out with a knife next time."

"It will be a matter of luck. It won't matter if you have the knife or not."

"He let me keep the food. I made the delivery."

Saturdays were for reading. Sundays through Fridays, for Wilbur Chiu. It was the barest of routines and he could feel, slowly, his anxiety slipping away. He continued to lift weights, keep his hair short, strengthen his legs through pedaling up hills, over curbs, between swerving trucks. There was a band of energy winding through him that had been unrecognizable. He didn't need the rush of coke. It was spring, it was summer. Chiu told him he could start delivering during the day.

"Sleep at night now."

"I don't mind the overnights."

"You'll start at noon."

"Okay, Mr. Chiu."

He learned the heat of afternoons, the frenzy beneath the train tracks and curbside on schooldays, the tidal roar of children freed from locked windows and instruction. He saw the massing outside the bodegas, firecrackers in the gutter, fingers dangling through chain-link fences as basketballs popped off speckled pavement. Queens, New York City. His hatred ebbed. He wasn't home—nothing, he was sure, could be that—but he had come to a place where he could remain. The urge to leave was vanishing. All he required was a bicycle and Chiu's money.

Tad had a habit of arriving early, twenty minutes or so before his shift, and the late morning was a slow time, Chinese food a rarer choice for breakfast. After flipping through his newspaper, Chiu would look up and rub his temples. Occasionally, when the mood struck, he would smoke a cigarette, a Marlboro red. The cloud hung over his eyes.

"Do you know what you're after?" he asked Tad.

"I don't."

"Every human has a moment of consciousness raising. A moment when they understand what it is they want."

"I don't understand it."

"You're here."

"Yes."

"This city takes more than it gives. Like this country. But you cling to what it is you have. You take it, screaming, into the grave. That, to me, is one dream."

"I like biking the afternoons. I'm glad you switched me."

"I knew you would."

"It's a new energy."

"You walk a city, you bike a city, especially an unfamiliar one, and you can feel the city rising to you. You feel the past, like a snake, wrapping around you. A city is an opportunity to meet more ghosts."

"I spent a lot of time in the country."

"Across America?"

"Rural towns. I lived in a cabin in a forest. I left it all behind."

"I came to America as a boy. I came here, to New York. New York was enough. New York was a threat and New York was an answer. I said I would make my money here and I did."

"I'm from New York. I left. Now I returned."

"America is many countries. That is what always worried me. That I would pass out of New York and into another land more foreign than any I had known, its customs alien, its demands deranged."

"When I lived in the cabin, I could feel myself flaking away. I would see my limbs fall off, my skin, my eyes. I would see myself as an invisible, hovering presence, without sight or mind. In the cabin I would dream."

"My wife, before she died, would say things like that too. She believed she was leaving herself behind."

"I never thought I was dying. I just felt this diminishing. Time and language, out of reach."

"She didn't think she was dying either."

Wilbur Chiu was the only person he spoke to for any length of time. In the library, he was alone with his microfilm. On the street, he pedaled onward, his lips pressed together. At home, he either read a book he had borrowed or slept. The couple next door fought with more ferocity as the summer wore on. He heard clattering, crying, the breaking of wood. He was increasingly certain the husband was menacing the wife, that there was a near-daily eruption of physical violence.

In fear, he sat and waited for the sounds to go away.

On the first Saturday in June, he found the archive of a defunct newspaper he had never heard of. It was a bellowing tabloid with tales of murders, sex, and political corruption. The name of the newspaper was the *Daily Raider* and the more he read of it, the more he began to understand it was unlike any newspaper. It was darker, odder, riven with conflict real and imagined, a newspaper operating on a more ferocious plane of engagement. Pigeons were slaughtered, for fun, at the gates of Prospect Park. A retired left-hander admitted to passing on his venereal disease to multiple women who weren't his wife. A neighborhood butcher believed he was the reincarnation of Adolf Hitler. Page after page, in blistering color, the headlines so bold that they seemed to punch at him through the microfilm. He began in the early 1970s and read as many editions as he could before the library closed.

"Do you remember the *Daily Raider*?" he asked Wilbur Chiu.

"It doesn't exist anymore."

"Yes. I found it in the library. I had no memory of it."

"It coursed through the city for a few years. It was a newspaper of blood and semen. That's how I thought of it. Everything that flows—the scum, the juice, the fluids that leak from meat. It was a newspaper for that part of existence. I make no judgment. That's just what it was."

"I read these old newspapers. I don't know why."

"They are selective reflections of the past, the collective memory that will soon be carried online. My son is very engaged with computers. He purchased one for me recently. He believes this will be the entirety of the future."

"I've never been much for computers."

"Think of the terminology. You go *on*line. You exist, here, *off*line. Language, I do believe, defines who it is we are, what we do. It is a form of destiny. A civilization is led to believe this sort of flesh world is *off* and only there, on your screen, are you on. We move in a way that begins to reject all it is we have been. Thousands of years turned to ash. Again, no judgment. You will learn, Tad, I don't do that."

It was on his second Saturday among the microfilm of the *Daily Raider* that he discovered their obsession with an entity named Vengeance. For long stretches of time, he was merely described. There were no photographs. Eyewitnesses said he wore a mask with two eye-slits. He preferred trench coats. Where were the photos? An article in 1974 stated that no newspaper, the Raider included, had photographed Vengeance. He liked to scrawl his name on walls and announce himself. The police were concerned because only the police could combat crime. "Vigilantism," said one police chief, "will not be tolerated in this city."

Vengeance started with broken up robberies. He beat, nearly lifeless, a gun-toting mugger. In time, he graduated to bigger game— finally, the beheading of an alleged serial rapist, rolling the skull out on 42nd Street, leaving it there for hungry and terrified and perplexed eyes. On the forehead, in his bright, slashing red paint: THIS IS VENGEANCE. Handwriting experts were called in to confirm it matched the graffiti. He was, Tad could tell, an anti-hero of near-classic vintage, stalking the night, hunting crime and snuffing it out. It seemed his conception was entirely informed by an earlier pop cultural moment. The urban backstreet brawlers. Here was one, come to life. The culture could do this. Though he had spent a decade disconnecting from it, shunning TV and cinema and comic books and radio, he had internalized enough from his first two decades of life to have a sense of how American ambition might manifest itself. We all wanted to be superheroes.

The NYPD had initiated a manhunt, dispatched officers across the city to catch this man who dared to wear a mask and do their job for them. "We believe he is psychotic," said a police captain in Manhattan. "We don't know what he's capable of. He does a good deed today, okay. What about tomorrow?" One day, the Raider was calling for Vengeance to be dragged in front of a court of law for daring "to do crimefighting outside the bounds of law." Other times, the editorial board would rally fully behind Vengeance's project : "The NYPD is clearly not up to the task. We demand safety and sanity in these dire times. If Vengeance can restore order, let him restore order."

Each story about Vengeance emphasized that he had never been photographed. There was a desperation to the coverage; it was an indignity that he had to be simply described, again and again, with insufficient language. The newspaper wanted to bring Vengeance to heel by photographing him. They wanted his reality on their front page. It was at a time when the image, at last, had achieved primacy over the written word, with TV ascendant and photographs in full color, their sophistication enough to render imagination irrelevant. Yet Vengeance was thriving, Tad saw, in this gap between imagination and reality. The more days passed without a photograph, the more powerful he became.

"Do you remember Vengeance?" he asked Chiu the following Friday.

"The vigilante."

"Yes."

"I remember there was a time when it felt like only mystical beings from the shadows could save us. I will tell you that I've been in America since I was a boy. But it is Americans who can grow most alienated from their country. Immigrants have a devotion to the ideal. The myth will always carry meaning. They came here, therefore they cannot be disappointed. To reject America is to reject yourself—the decisions you made, what your essence became."

"I'm trying to understand."

"Vengeance arrived at a very specific point in history, and many silently cheered him on. I was well into my thirties, my financial station secure. We tasted anarchy and saw him as an agent against it."

"One man against anarchy, huh? I'm not sure I buy it."

"Vengeance was a fundamentally conservative figure. He was here for restoration. He was here to bring us what we believed we had before, but never had."

The following Saturday, Tad found the newspaper he was waiting for. On the front page of the *Daily Raider*, there was nothing else. THIS IS VENGEANCE. The photograph was close, in greater detail and resolution, if that was the right word, than he imagined it would be. The cloth mask and the two slits for eyes were clear enough to him to gaze into, to strain, through two decades, to understand. Half of the newspaper was dedicated to Vengeance, celebrating, in part, the Raider's coup, with retrospectives assembled in haste, as if he had died. The myriad "exclusives" indicated they had defeated the competition. He sensed, knowing little of the newspaper's trajectory, this was the apex of the *Raider*. There would never be glory again like this and this made him unhappy, that life had been set in such a way.

According to the newspaper, the photographer had taken the image of Vengeance as he attacked her, trying to reach through the window of a car. He remembered his father telling him when he was young that most of life was luck and timing. It was a phrase his father often repeated, to almost musical effect. Luck and timing. For a long time, he thought he understood what it meant. The best and worst is due to chance: when you show up, what happens when you do. He had felt neither in his own life. Comprehension was theoretical. Only now, delivering for Chiu and sifting through newspapers in the library, did he begin to approach his father's words with any kind of permanent understanding.

Certain people believe they migrate through life under a lucky star and he had never been one of those people. He never had a reason to be. Now, for the first time, he could believe there was meaning in his return. His timing, once off, was now on. He continued to read.

The photographer interviewed Vengeance on the telephone. He would not reveal his identity. It was unlike anything he had ever read.

There are layers of hell and I am below them, between them.

This city is failing. You can feel it. I can feel it. We all believe in it, still, we collectively will it to life, each and every day. But for how long? How long can we dream? How long will you dream? Ultimately, I am for order over chaos, matter over anti-matter, creation over negation. The New York Police Department, which I know intimately, is a failed state. It is the Ottoman Empire on the eve of the Great War. It has exhausted itself. I step into the breach. London Bridge is falling down. Falling down, falling down. London Bridge is falling down, my fair lady.

Carrying the words with him, he couldn't help but share them with Chiu before his next shift. When he entered the takeout restaurant, Chiu was scrubbing the countertop, whistling an unidentifiable tune.

"I read an interview with Vengeance," Tad said.

"I remember it."

"What he said?"

"How I felt about it."

"They are words unlike any I've read."

"It was unlike any time I had lived through."

"He sang a song."

"London Bridge."

"You remember."

Chiu lit a cigarette, settling into a thin folding chair behind the counter. He sat like an old-world monarch in repose, his fist balanced beneath his chin, his eyes drifting to a corner of light only he could see. He exhaled, the smoke traveling slowly from his mouth. "His identity was never found out. The police couldn't find him. Neither could any newspaper."

"The song was a clue."

"Yes."

"How could no one find him?"

"Those who don't want to be found don't get found. I believe this. There is no better place to hide than New York City."

"He changed his name?"

"From old to new."

"How do you know?"

"Everyone who wanted to know could know. For all the fulminating of the police, the newspapers, I am not sure they wanted to know. There is more interest in potentiality. There is a chase afoot. No one really wants to know what they are chasing. Once Vengeance falls into custody, the story ends. If he disappears, he can still be out there. Enough time passes and he becomes unreal. He retreats into myth. The New York Police Department can be forgiven for never apprehending a myth."

"I imagine he is still out there."

"You are thinking of him now."

"I imagine he is close to us, Mr. Chiu. I imagine he is past fifty, gray at the temples, beginning to slump. He has a small apartment in Bayside, among the retiring Jews. He goes to the deli for a turkey on rye. He has packed his past away."

"Or he embraces it."

"Maybe he remembers all of it. Maybe he writes his name in his own blood. The apartment is wrecked, mutilated, beyond recognition. It has the odor of wartime. He still sings 'London Bridge.'"

Vengeance slowly disappeared from the *Raider*. There were more stories about eyewitnesses and police leads, crimes foiled. No one else, as far as Tad could tell, photographed him. As the 1970s wore on, there were other creatures of the night to occupy the newspaper. Marauding homeless. Hijacked subway cars. Son of Sam. It was as Chiu said. He had retreated.

It was a noble idea. A single person to stand against disorder. Put on a mask and drop into the night. Vengeance, for a moment, permitted the culture of fantasy to meet the brutality of every day.

Chiu seemed to understand.

The summer was long and hot. His legs and forearms were browned and muscled, his shirt tight against his back, the sweat staining and drying and staining again. He was careening through Queens midday, straining to beat his own times. Twelve minutes to 77th Street, six minutes to 30th Avenue, fourteen to the BQE. He saved all of his money but what he put toward rent and electricity and occasional grocery trips. His cash tips were filed in the drawer of a desk he had found on the sidewalk and carried upstairs. He had worked, on and off, since he was sixteen, and this was the first time the money mattered to him. It was labor vital, somehow, to who he was.

At the end of August, he biked from Queens through Brooklyn, streaking south. He would make the beach. At Coney Island, he collapsed in a small cloud, his lips dry. He was laughing. He lay his bike in the sand. Seagulls circled overhead. He had not eaten all day. A sand-caked canteen was drained. He could see the parachute jump in the corner of his eye, enormous and flowering. Boomboxes thudded with music he never learned. A volleyball arced over his outstretched body. Up above, the sky was streaked with white clouds, a passenger jet threading in and out of sight.

He hadn't come here since he was a child; he remembered his mother referring to Coney Island as a slum.

The memory trickled out of him. He closed his eyes, allowing his mind to void itself. He tried not to think at all. The surf pulled in and out, the salty foam hissing. He felt the sun deep in his skin. He understood why people came here. He unbuttoned his shirt and lay in the hot sand in his shorts, letting his body gather heat.

In early September, having reached the end of his *Daily Raider* newspapers, he decided to skip his trip to the library. Instead, he wandered into Blue Star, where Chiu was smoking a cigarette and painting the walls. He had settled on a dark red, almost maroon. The paint had a distinct and dizzying smell.

"You decided to repaint."

"Have you ever made a decision without knowing why it was made for you?"

"Yes."

"There is a liberating aspect. Body and mind are not in their arranged marriage. That is a trick of Eastern and Western civilization, that both should be together. That they deserve to be joined."

"A mind free of a body. And a body free of a mind."

"A body that moves, unimpeded, undertakes the purest form of action. Unclouded by thought. Unclouded by societal rot. Action for the sake of action."

"That could lead to violence."

"Violence as purification."

"Did Vengeance believe in that?"

"Vengeance believed that he alone could deliver a society free of sin. He was an idealist. Under the strain, he disappeared."

"I want to find him."

Chiu stopped painting. He looked up toward the ceiling.

"Vengeance couldn't accept he would be born into the world that he would die in," Chiu said.

Tad delivered on all seven days at the start of September, 2001. On the eighth day, he delivered again. On the ninth, he decided he would go out once more.

"I don't need a day off," he told Chiu.

Chiu grunted at him.

The tenth, Tad decided, would be the last before his break. It was a Monday. He would work Monday and sleep deeply on Tuesday. He informed Chiu of his plan.

"When you sleep on Tuesday, let yourself dream."

He did.

5 Poems From
The Flowing Light of the Film's End
Emmalea Russo

Extreme Close-Up

on white powder beach
days cling to days

lost in the place above

garden of mirth
where did our terrace go?

your eyes were rough crystals
I saw the simplest

images through
bowls of drugs in the truss

we rushed through
Earthly Paradise into who?

up and backward
toward another foyer

crude and virtual
Saint Bernard tells us

to look closer
at what we think we see

people seated in the rose
spun by cupidity

mad and fast into an atrium
at whose center sits a wayfarer worthier

but I was unsound and loud
a lover

flitting in this pink
and purple swimsuit

around hotel grounds

lulled
to sleep by engines

thrusting sunward
carrying

words maybe

The Saint Hotel

Between the beach and The Saint Hotel

violet white waves under
storm-tonsured sky
void my head
end
end

yeah I've loved men
of action and violence
plague-pleasant

like Wallace Stevens
as his fist shot
toward a novelist

in Florida

a decade before Bogie drove
skinny overseas highway
tinsel and glimmer

I, sundumb
enter the hotel on a day

high as Hemingway

at a cocktail party
I send an email then watch
one translucent palm sway

in totality-blue
flanked by signs
I send you

what I send you

THE SAINT HOTEL
CRYSTAL BALL
SWIMMING POOL

is this the palm at the end
of my mind or
a tree emptied

of images
of itself
above a zenithless

blown-out gulf
dazzling into tranquility
or not, no?

I phone the blotch
of white which is the sun
no storms none

a Victorian novel big and unfinishable
sweats against my stomach
on a white bench between sand

and pastel hotel I eat and drink
the clear sweets of paradise
junk and vapor on the street

etheromania and Florida
sun eats your electronic words
gunning under me I FIGHT DEMONS
reads a man's shirt *waiting to be seated?*
clouds in the sky? zero
visibility? *I don't know who you are*
frameless cobalt freaked with clear
deleting an art deco steeple
an idea of order
a heady line

from Wallace Stevens

as I reach

stoned
for my phone
to tell you something good
but the light got it first, *so*

I can hear the rusted gate of Paradise
thinning as someone quotes Tennyson
nodding off into chlorine and tin
devouring ice cream, cake, Coke
as we smoke the air fills-in
with *Sturm und Drang*
and shakes iridescent
a pelican lands on my sternum
pulls from my hips a gift

where can I redeem this?

remind me please
why did I come
stunned
to the bottom
of the country
and is the garden
still above?

the shadow of the palm
is a gun
I'm inside of

propellant
against asphalt

metal *come
down here, fait accompli*

your hand is where
the pelican
was
just
it's midday
as it'll always
be

no
you asshole

it's neither question
nor philosophy

neither poem
nor autobiography

neither therapy
nor abduction fantasy
but flu-inducing

reality

I try to eat
the big books

of paradise

under silver cans
sibilant and spinning

so fast
no motion
can be detected

huh?

huh?

cupped by voices
exquisitely quotidian

hi. hello.
how are you?

fine, you?
uh. uh.

Mallọmar sun coats
the scene in cream and I ask

over a lit page of Stevens
and his palm tree

why are you doing this to me?

I drive into town
as needle palm greens
congregate

around *one* of me

the other one
is wind-whipped
masted
and foggy

who may I ask is calling?

Terra

In the cream hotel suite
I spent all my light

Begun again to spin what you said
Over in my head and hand and the hands

Of other dwellers but we'd been
Going toward oblivion

had it been
fuck!
minutes, months???

Souls adorning the air
Stripping memory to

Bone-white glare
On the Victorian terrace

Flipping through images of
Gospel figures, you were barely

There

But still showed me a painting of
The Road to Calvary *where is the light*

Coming from you wondered
As the terrace turned

Meth-white clouds
Fused the room to

Great Expectations

Certain medieval beliefs held that Adam was not born in Eden.

But in the opposite Eden.

Eden,

a dream we belonged to
pronged, meant to be visitors
never occupants, permanent tints

In Nabokov's novel *Ada, or Ardor: A Family Chronicle* (1969), which spans one-hundred years, Van and Ada are siblings and lovers who spend their time in a garden not unlike Eden and its sibling-lovers Eve and Adam. In the novel, the estate is called Ardis Manor.

At the next turning, the romantic mansion appeared on the gentle eminence of old novels. Turning, a mansion is letters and weather. Whether the siblings are there or not, Ardis appears in their minds as miniature, green, ravine-filled, twinkling.

Ada will show you all the rooms in the house.

Boring. Happiness being notoriously uncapturable. In Nabokov's novel, Paradise is ground intractable, decorated and thick with River Ladore and I am not yet a lapsed Catholic.

There are twin planets:

Antiterra (Daemonia)
Terra

A hair away from our world, Terra may exist only as a hallucination in the minds of Antiterra residents. Terra is the other world and the other world gets confused and conflated *by sick minds* with this world and the next world, the afterworld. *In us as it's behind and above us.*

Vatic, spurious, adhering to an ancient sprung-up formula mystic-scientific. Van wants to prove the state of mind (Terra) and the place (Terra) are the same. Boxes labeled HELL and boxes labeled HEAVEN got all mixed-up.

Today, a movie sun runs the zodiac
industrious, busy, flowery computer-
blue-green. I email, then call. The dial
tone is brand new as the light variously
sits and glides, outdoes my mind. Finally,
green totality. OK, we meet. Both of us
seventeen and weirdly quoting Andrew Marvell's poetry:

Annihilating all that's made
To a green thought in a green shade.

In Nabokov's novel, a young Ada attempts to translate Andrew
Marvell's poem "The Garden" into French. The pretty green
mansion I'm in, in which happiness enters me. I do not care that
the structure is apparently devoid of architectural integrity, that it
mixes old forms with new, is a symbol of something-or-other, and
is, according to him, luxuriously ugly. You do not care, either. It's a
mansion that took us in, though, as you insist, all homes are tem-
porary. Some green tints are permanent, I say. "Secret Garden," for
instance, from the Sherwin-Williams website.

But this mansion, Florida-green, shrinks into something which,
when we suck on it, makes us chemical-batshit. After happiness
passes, I'm mad with candy-green joy which points towards my
words as they fail, fall. The air is black with gnats, a buzzing film
between you and me, baroque with humidity. The last overgrown
decades of the 19th century are still sweating on a tummy. The old
house is restored. *Christina's World* hangs above a computer on the
fritz. There's a quake whenever a soul changes floors. I spit green.

Bliss?

In *Return of the Native* (1878) Thomas Hardy describes the strangely
familiar scenery of Egdon Heath where stretches of whitish clouds
swing and disperse over whitish sky and heaven does not open but
instead spreads over the world proving it's a screen placed pallidly
over changing states.

In *Great Expectations* (1861), Miss Havisham lives in opposite
paradise: a sham mansion with a paused altar. All day it's twenty
minutes to nine.

In the English novel, Havisham is aged because there is no sun.

In the 1998 movie adaptation, set along Florida's gulf coast, Anne
Bancroft's Havisham got too much sun.

Film and novel unfurl
along marshes between
water and land. Paradise
and its opposite cross
at the gulf
still
altered
what's set apart
seeps and speaks
film set with book
droning, droning
silver jets blow
over the wet meadow
gobsmacked, *I've got nothing*
neither wit nor innocence
to share with you, just
enervation, verveless
On the train, I read
about euthanasia
and Aristotle's
idea of soul
then watch
Great Expectations (1998) where

PARADISO PERDUTO

is the name of Havisham's mansion

PARADISO PERDUTO

reads the rusted gate

PARADISE LOST

I desire, in Florida, to visit the mansions that I was promised years
ago in surges by certain books and movies. Inside every garden,

anti-garden
ardent earth
hardening thin
strip of green
separating gulf
from ocean
a city of palms undulating
over hotel pool and reflected
in the black electronic baths
of our phones

i thicken
a palm see-saws
all of hell resounds
yes — astonished
did you choose this?

Ca' d'Zan (House of John) is the name of the mansion used as the filming location for PARADISO PERDUTO, Miss Havisham's house in the movie adaptation. At the edge of the gulf, water is silky green-white and hot. Built in the 1920s, Ca' d'Zan was the winter residence of circus mogul John Ringling.

I've been here before. Back when I wrote this down, all of the above and what comes after, in this way exactly. And how?

Turquoise sky against turquoise eyes. Who's mad now, huh?!

I sweat. The air is ornament.

Oh, we say, and then, *oh.* Then: nothing at all.

A desire moving so fast it's unrecognizable.

A circus ring parodies
Paradise's breeze
shook the trees
but there was nothing
no wind
just a green screen
with green

In the novel, Havisham's residence is SATIS HOUSE. *Enough already, enough. OK. OK.* On the gulf, I get sick. There is the mansion, twisted.

CA' D'ZAN, John and Mable Ringling's Gothic mansion sits on the edge of white water, bequeathed to the state in 1939.

In *Key Largo*, Bogie drove south along the road, throat-like and buckling under the approaching storm.

Today at the manse at the edge of the whirl,
I visit John and Mable's graves tucked away
near bamboo woods and I could give it all up for

nothing much, which is *Paradiso*'s dazzling interior
heaven's flashiest part gothic and plucked
from parts of Europe then planted here

at the edge of Florida under sun we split, conjoin,
split, mix again in the spit-like whitewater
at gulf's start effervescing into suds

Hi, thinking of you
madly i'm your
Gothic style
divine sense where
you know less
a superlative
that is beyond
whatever the palms
reach for

just say normal things,
my nerves my nerves ok!
fried, how are you
and yours what did you eat
how was your day what
if anything did you make

Mais ou sont les neiges d'antan
light and color press against each other
marry the stained glass windows

of Ca' d'Zan, an emanation diffusing
as it reaches we who stand waiting
on the bay as shapes curving

at gothic pace
love's daring
extinguished Cavalcanti Dante

and Ringling's circus poetry
a procession
then the everyday

surveillance of angels
ministers of another economy
I get super

affixed to you plus
whatever sounds images
pour through the machine

for reaching you
in mansion's
liquid shadow

zodiacal mosaic
tourists
spindle palm
walls from the room
in which *The Decameron*
was written
knotty pine
Wunderkammers

February thaws
over chalk scribble
of lack and loveliness and Jesus
on macadam ardently
a contradictory transcendence
I was ready to give it all up
but what was *it*
and where was *up*
perched above

usual language
superancient
another sun or you
past perfect
beside the hotel pool
i quote you
then again in the lobby
sunsick
I phone you
quiet and quick
our respective edges
click click click
you're in the urinal
I become a channel
standing in the foyer
of the Floridian multiplex
near the pen you write
your treatise with
I don't give a shit
It was fucked up what you did

In the 1998 movie adaptation of *Great Expectations*, PARADISO
PERDUTO is hidden in overgrowth. To prepare for filming, they
faked this part, adding neglect, decay, mildew, and moss to the man-
icured House of John. Junk under the orange sun bouncing off turquoise sky which matches clean the water it hovers over and floats,
flotsam. Blots it out. Off. Roland Barthes uses the word *paradise*
but twice in *A Lover's Discourse*. The first time, the word is enclosed
within gate-like parentheses. *Power* on one side, *dream* on the other.

The second time, *paradise* floats outside the place the lover gets
expelled from as, thanks to language, she becomes her own demon.
Ejects and invites Legion images in and in. To injure, inure. I'll see
you at the pool. Airplanes and pelicans.

despair, jealousy, fear,
nature's dis
order, the endless static
of language pro-
and re-

and un-
and
and
um

Those demons, once angels, are so *experienced*, stuffed with knowledge after falling back, a relapse. From the light a pelican flies
under. *Sigh*—but *no*, dives down, *hmm? huh???* The demon finally
convulses as I walk toward the mansion across the highway, suddenly northern and storied as that house in *Christina's World*.

PARADISE

Parenthetical and severed
language or each other
what in the end covers
gulf coast soaks
beat-up Victorian novels
ashore, books stack up
matte and sturdy
they do not record me
they do not record me

I consult the Victorians, my own sternum, dirt, sturdier objects
filled with words and the demonic birds that carry them up and
away before dropping them *thud splash fuck* off the skinniest coast

soon i'll arrive wordless
in the desert
carrying three books
arid, drawn-on
turbulent and red
how was the ride?
who did you sit beside?
what did you look at, watch, read?
carousel spins
as the sun bloats
where've you been?
sickened and stuffed
with words
days go by like

can't find the time
so list the gated places
houses decayed or upkept
here's my thigh
all of the above dunked
in River Lethe
can i get a ride

Daemonia
Ardis Manor
Egdon Heath
Satis House
Ca' d'Zan
Paradise Gone
repeat x3
xo, E

We two kids in the hottest garden

In Florida at the end of February

Wrapped in lightweight gold and enclosed

A dash above us which is the sun

Mold-green and churchy

Stun-gunned, imparadised

I was a medieval virtue retold

In a Victorian novel then dripped into the humidest

Piece of America

Once-vaulted planets now move

By what force I was thrown here, and *whose*

I don't know, though *it spoke*

I was cleaned of dreams

Undriven to speak or repeat

White light without screen

I will leave this place having never read for instance

Euripides, Parmenides, lesser-known novel of Dickens and Hardy

"IT OPENED TO THE GROUND, AND LOOKED INTO
A MOST MISERABLE CORNER OF THE NEGLECTED
GARDEN, UPON A RANK RUIN OF CABBAGE-STALKS,
AND ONE BOX TREE THAT HAD BEEN CLIPPED
ROUND LONG AGO, LIKE A PUDDING, AND HAD A NEW
GROWTH AT THE TOP OF IT, OUT OF SHAPE AND OF A
DIFFERENT COLOUR......."

Inside out, didn't think to train for light without heat
nor heat without light *the train ride home was long
and cold, shot through edges of towns i could barely make out*,
conductor said *tickets out tickets out, then hey you, you*
and at the end, froths of gulf that might've been worn out
from the trip
w of wings
    of whatever
affixed to things
newer with nothing much
to brush up against, everything
suddenly winged *I'm in a garden now
and now? Florida? California?* then
*huh! where is this? there are two rivers
and a chariot. there is persistence of vision
and all is cinema!?*
Miss Havisham repents late
but perhaps not *too* late
for eventual entrance
into Paradise, right
*back in gulf water again,
and now, now
Los Angeles*
Norma Desmond
stuck in drugged
light, frozen and in-
camera'd flashing

into th'other place
which is this one
unsung and singed
with weariness
The Garden
precut
by a screen-
like lake
residues
leftovers
plagues
clean
dissociative
aloof, a little
Ketamine
good, good,
sweet, but
this thing is leaking

I found a book
Mass market, half-dissolved
Brought it to Florida

Between WILD PALMS and OLD MAN
tongue-and-groove *DARK WIND FILLED WITH THE WILD DRY*
SOUND OF PALMS

The veil between us *was going now, dissolving now, it was about to part*
now and now

Gone—
my veil was of synthetic material
1980s elaborate gold sparkle
and translucent diffusing the light
I am a former ice skater in heels walking
over a floor of words under revolving lot
Hissed in the harsh salt grass of the unkempt other lot
after the ceremony, I mingle, wondering
why bring self here, gold-drenched to ride OF ALL PLACES TO SEA
LEVEL?

I sprint toward *FULL SWEEP OF UNIMPEDED SEA-WIND*
WHICH THRASHED AMONG UNSEEN PALMS AND invisibly
longed to be a person who makes things
which do not bend in the wind
but which the wind
bends to

Palms hurl themselves upward only to break *antic on the wall*
shot back into the place we first met, a crystal-ball *near dry clashing*
of invisible palms

I have requested a sewing kit from the front desk
I am going to fix this
Then read every psalm in my gold dress

I will sit and stare *THAT KNOCKING SOUND AGAIN AT ONCE*
DISCREET AND PEREMPTORY you message me from a paused
song as fronds clap the window
my hand, shaking, threads a silver needle

Hey, remember that day
at the arcade? at the state's
edge, a miracle or a mirage
birdsong
birdsong
not sad but fire-
fangled Floridian
evening I ostensibly
see you in but no–
you're on the other side
neverminded, nothing
I can take it, yeah! bye.
The palm in the middle, stringent
begins to spin and Bacall and Bogie
in *Key Largo* reach toward each other

I enter the crude foyer
I sway in the lobby
in the regular way
feathers shining
in a birdcage

human feeling
of mere being
between me and
are you okay?

Wind turns bronze then gold
6:14am— *i'm sorry, who?*

Key Largo (1948)

Emm? you said
Like I was dead

After I ran on hot gray
Asphalt around Tampa Bay

The sun clicking
Above chaise lounge

I stick to
And miraculously

You said
Emmmmmm?

Where the islands disappear
Into *that's not sea*
Nor sand
But something else
Entirely
Bogie drives on
Cutting thru the gray
Hour hand
Stops
Per usual pissed off
Deserted house
At the end
Of ardor
Disease
Like its beginning
Stinks
The light goes

Matte gray
Sulfurous
Unglimmering
This is a movie
Of hotels and houses
Screaming people
In pieces

I return to the delirium
Backed by Florida gray
Before the blue of day
Where you are Bogie
And I'm Bacall desaturated
And reaching across
Coasts sartorially
If I could only convince you
But no
PSYCHIC
DANGER
Melted bumper sticker
Peeling off big black car
In pristine driveway
Sky's blue again
Psychopomp
Vomiting up
The whole crew
Wheezing
Dilapidated
Then blistered
Into new

The Body Cam Heiress

Anna Krivolapova

Roman Abosch went fully gray at twenty-six. He learned to be grateful for it. It reminded him that time was always running out. He finished school at twenty-four and engineered military antennae before pivoting to cameras. Roman surprised himself—he had no interest in photography outside of its archaeological purpose. He started Lupine Security and lobbied competing body camera technology into obsolescence. His company owned a monopoly over law enforcement video equipment in thirty-seven states and had security guards stationed on every block of coastal Georgia, Florida, and California. Resorts, boardwalks, waterfronts, and parks were fully stocked with Roman's rent-a-cops. They were trained to be friendly, approachable, and treat every nodding, fleabitten, pungent vagrant with dignity. Never yell, never be condescending, and speak to everyone like a friend. Speak like every single word they say is being recorded, transcribed, and stored in an office building full of servers in Prince William County, Virginia. Some of the guards worked in pseudo-plain clothes that drew a strange reaction. The men in bright white Under Armour had a mildly hypnotic effect on schizophrenics and the "white army" had been mistaken for everything from angels to Mormons. They were especially effective crime deterrents in the South and Pacific Northwest.

Roman and his daughter watched some footage from a Cub store in St. Paul. Two security guards patrolling the parking lot politely asked a homeless woman to return her shopping cart and find another place to sleep. She peeled a flannel shirt off a basket of sleeping puppies and asked the guards for some change to buy milk. The runt was dying. The older guard crouched down and asked her where she found them. She said their mother was hit by a car and she had delivered the puppies from her corpse. The younger guard did not show any fear or disgust on his face, and asked if she knew to massage their stomachs after feeding them. She nodded and blurted out *of course* but looked embarrassed, and started vigorously petting the colicky runt. The interaction was friendly, but she turned hostile when they offered her a ride to the women's shelter. *The homeless endure the longest days but enjoy the shortest lives*, Roman thought.

PJ Abosch, the surveillance magnate's only child, was a tall seventeen year old with straight blonde hair and long muscular legs. When she came home from school, her father would usually be in their basement theater watching footage from work. He would pat the couch cushion next to him and ask her to weigh in. She would sit on the floor too close to the TV, still in her field hockey uniform and clogs with ugly socks, identical to all the other girls at her vaguely Christian all-girls high school. Holt Academy was a small Quaker school of only twenty-nine girls per grade. Most of the students were quiet religious girls with mousy hair they were never allowed to cut, or, seemingly, brush. Once in a while, there would be a new girl who PJ and the other private school veterans could tell had been kicked out of entire public school districts. They usually had fake dark hair, like it used to be pink or blue and they had to cover it to make Holt's dress code. Sometimes they had scars on their faces where eyebrow, lip, or nose piercings used to be. They depressed PJ. They reminded her of craft store cashiers in matte blue aprons. Those ex-alt girls tended to quietly vanish after a few weeks of being shunned by the Wicker Man faction in their long kilts and cardigans buttoned to the top. Holt gave all the girls straight A's and a nice warm pizza-paddle transfer into good colleges. The school's lax curriculum and PJ's precocious puberty that extended into a high verbal IQ had convinced her family that she was a genius.

Her father was beta testing a new lens that made the footage a little fisheyed and disturbingly high definition. She could see tears welling in people's eyes while they were crumbling under police questioning. She started to recognize the same people being arrested over and over again, usually for sleeping rough, or in their cars.

"They say this new lens is supposed to increase empathy for law enforcement." Roman began. "What do you think?"

He waited for his daughter's response but she was entranced by the bodycam footage playing on their TV. She didn't flinch as a homeless man in a wife beater cried out in pain and confusion while getting tased by the police, even though the inevitability of the man's death from the beginning of the clip made Roman feel bloated with dread. His daughter was braver. She never averted her gaze from the overdoses, suicides by cop, drunk women getting tased and soiling their tight party dresses in front of a busy nightclub. When these scenes came on, he preferred to turn away and watch her reactions. It amazed him how little her face changed, mouth slightly agape like a little girl's, belly on the sheepskin rug.

"I think it looks too much like a video game," she finally answered. "It makes their jobs look like too much fun. Cops get to have this release valve that everyone else can't touch. Everyone else has to stay pent up all the time."

"I'll pull it tomorrow."

PJ was known to tell a moving story about a homeless man who used to harass her at the bus stop every day. She talked about living in fear until she watched the body cam footage of his last moments, which were spent cornering a lone cop in a quiet cul-de-sac. She recounted watching him wield a knife at the deputy and commit suicide by cop. *Every victim deserves that peace of mind.*" She told this story at a fundraising dinner or three, no matter how many present guests knew that Miss Abosch had never set foot inside a bus. She was hardly allowed to leave Roman's gated mansion with cameras in every hallway. The story was something she overheard from a classmate, a Polish girl with a grown out shag and empty stretched earlobes that hung limp, reminding PJ of a squeamish part of male anatomy. Justyna was adopted by rich parents whom she constantly disavowed. She came to the US at age seven and claimed she had been stolen from her grandparents and sold to Russian child traffickers. PJ liked to eavesdrop on Justyna's outlandish stories, which were sadly all true. Justyna got expelled from Holt for taking ketamine and falling asleep in the courtyard with her skirt flipped up. Her arrest was some of PJ's favorite footage.

Since asking her parents for permission to go out with her friends was like applying for a visa, PJ spent most of her time online. She didn't like social media. It made her envy her peers who were allowed to have sleepovers, movie dates, and ski trips. They were allowed to drive their own cars, have boyfriends, and choose their own clothes. But envy was beneath her. She preferred to scroll through mugshots, inmate rosters, and the sex offender registry.

Once in a while, there would be a special person among the usual meth heads and neanderthals, an attractive person with nice skin and life in their eyes. This would be their one and only mugshot they take in their life. It'll be a joke to them. They'll print it out and tape it to their fridge to get a rise out of their friends at dinner parties. They smirk or purse their lips or even wink. Sometimes you can tell they are familiar with the person behind the camera through a warmth in their eyes, where their pupils are focused. She didn't know what she was looking for in all those faces until she saw Jason Cotton, a handsome felon with an impressive array of crimes as well as neck and face tattoos.

In his mugshots, Cotton looked humbled and a little scared. He looked like he didn't expect to get caught. Handsome but not cocky about it. There was a modicum of remorse in the corner of his mouth. PJ liked the tufts of cotton tattooed on his neck. Family pride. If she ever got a tattoo, she'd lose her family's respect forever. She looked over his crimes. *Forged prescriptions, theft of controlled substances, battery.* She saw a lot of *battery* without really knowing what it meant. It seemed boring without the "sexual" prefix. She skimmed over the list, thinking she could just ask him about it later. She was pleased to see his prison was less than an hour away without traffic, and started looking for a way to call him. She squirreled Roman's computer up to her bedroom to use his facial recognition software and see if any of Jason's arrests had been recorded by Lupine, but did not find a match.

*

Ari Roth was her father's attorney and best friend of 32 years. Ari was a short, stocky tank with a receding hairline. He wasn't the type of balding man to shave his head— he let his thick dark curls grow in a mane that continued all over his chest, legs, and in between. He reminded PJ of a satyr when she watched him wrestle the junior associates in his law firm's rugby club. They had always been close throughout her childhood, and he had always looked the same. She saw pictures of him as a teen and he was balding then too. PJ had speedrun puberty as well. It ran in the family. She couldn't ever recall looking down and just seeing a flat chest.

Ari came into the house to greet Roman and Greta. In his warm, confident, deep voice, he told them he was picking her up and hosting her for the night so she could borrow one of his cars for a school field trip in the morning. Roman was too strict and too stingy to get a third car for PJ, even though he could easily afford it. The story was dubious but Roman was distracted with revolutionizing policing by developing a solution to one of the more cumbersome aspects of the body cams: storage. Police departments were spending more on digital storage than the cameras themselves. Lupine was developing a database to replace the videos. Each video would be analyzed by facial recognition software and replaced with plain text files containing social security numbers, license plates, and addresses, along with a description of the video. This was only done for the more mundane moments caught on camera, like parking ticket disputes. Fights, shootings, and police chases stayed. There was a small demand for hard copies of juicy footage, which made Roman raise an eyebrow. He didn't want to be named in some X-dossier. His daughter assured him it was just tabloids. The tabloids had really changed since he was younger. Gone were the days of paparazzi and tasteful sex scandals. This generation wants beheadings and street brawls.

PJ pulled up the footage of Justyna's arrest at Ari's house. She carried his projector down into the indoor pool to watch it on the large wall of pale blue tiles. First her phone, now the TV was too small for it. She wanted to be immersed. Ari watched her with a cocked eyebrow. She was about to get his projector wet. He watched her sink back into the pool while the video began. It was body cam footage from police coming upon a young schoolgirl with a mullet haircut lying face down in a school courtyard. She wore a navy blue cardigan, plaid kilt, and dark lace underwear. She was barefoot and laying on a windbreaker she used as a makeshift blanket. A poodle haired teacher was wringing her hands, afraid to touch her.

"Watch this," PJ whispered. She liked the cop's tan arms reaching for Justyna's white unconscious legs. With a quick motion, he flipped her skirt to its correct position to protect her modesty. "I like it when he does that," PJ said, entranced. She started to rewind the video over and over to make it look like the cop was undressing her. "He hasn't even felt her pulse yet. She could be dead here. He doesn't even know if she's alive, but he fixes her skirt."

Ari stayed in the hot tub, trying not to look, worried that PJ had come over to show him another snuff video. "PJ, how does it end? Don't show me any weird shit today, okay? Always watching these videos can't be healthy."

"Wait—watch. She goes apeshit on Mrs. Groenman."

The cop tapped Justyna on the shoulder and loudly asked her if she needed medical attention. She mumbled and curled into her jacket, hiding her eyes. The policeman asked an EMT to help pick her up. Mrs. Groenman slid her hands under Justyna's armpits to save her from being manhandled by the cops but the girl woke up and grabbed her beaded glasses cord. After she broke the cord and lost her leverage, she started grabbing handfuls of her teacher's hair. The police flipped her back onto her stomach and handcuffed her, during which you got another glimpse of her panties. Her face contorted into a panicked grimace and she begged for them not to send her to the psych ward. She listed three of them off by name.

"Anything but Mt. Sinai. Please. I'll go back to class."

"Too late," the faceless male voice replied.

"Let me go, I'm just a kid."

PJ paused the video and turned to see Ari's reaction. She had a post-orgasmic flush on her cheeks and neck. The way she inhaled, he knew she was about to start talking for a long while if he didn't give her an opinion quickly enough. He was equally aroused and disgusted by what she had just shown him. He wondered if he'd feel differently if the girl had looked like PJ, blonde with huge curves and just enough baby fat. The girl in the video had a nice body and decent face ruined by a rebellious haircut and mania.

"I'm going to show you another one. This one is *good*. Don't tell my dad but I kind of sold it to Worldstar and made three hundred dollars." It was endearing to him how excited she was about that amount of money. It made him curious about the video.

"Hollywood Boulevard. You know, that sidewalk with the stars. Get this—they made it illegal to sit down. So every time someone sits down, they get a talking-to from security guards. My dad and I watched hours of this. Just two guys walking around telling people to stand up. It's usually kinda boring and depressing. Old people, homeless, crazy starfuckers. This one guy started telling the cops he was a member of Stone Temple Pilots, saying *'you better let me go before I miss my show. We're playing at the Hollywood Bowl later.'* They almost believed him, but then he started yelling other stuff. Almost the exact same stuff as Justyna was saying when she was arrested. Watch."

She put on a video of a middle-aged man sitting cross-legged on the ground with a zip tie holding his wrists behind his back. His short hair and tanned skin were almost the same shade of bronze. He rocked back and forth, oscillating between insults and flattery, trying every strategy he could to win back his freedom. Seven other cops stood around him in a semicircle.

"Look at what he's about to say." PJ leaned forward, clearly having memorized the video.

"Don't touch me, I'm a minor!" he cried out. "Don't tase me! Are you private or LAPD? Please be LAPD. Don't tase me again. You tased me last week. Please send me to Twin Town, not the other ones. Anything but Resnick."

"Do you think he really meant that? *I'm a minor*? You think he doesn't know how old he is?"

"He's just trying to get let off."

"It's deeper than that. I have a theory."

"What's your theory?" Ari asked, weary of theory. "How do you watch *hours* of this?"

"I think they're ex-child actors who got drugged and pimped out until they could no longer perform. They tend to be handsome, with big blue eyes and a nice jaw. Good bone structure, has potential, but too vulnerable. Totally frozen in time from abuse. Like when women on Forensic Files have that super high-pitched voice and you can tell they got—"

"What are you gonna do, start a nonprofit like your mom? *Save the Gen X meth heads from the Hollywood pedo elite?*"

"Yes," PJ laughed. "And you and my dad are going to give me a million dollars to do it."

Ari turned off the projector and took it far away from the pool. He dried off and stretched out on his sectional in a terry bathrobe with a busy Missoni print. His chest hair reflected the blinking glow of the TV. PJ's head was in his lap as they watched a movie that they both agreed did not deserve that year's Oscar.

"Ari, I need a favor."

"Anything."

"Can I use your letterhead for something?"

Ari just laughed. "Who are you trying to intimidate?"

"It's for a school project. I need to visit a prisoner and interview them."

"What class is this?"

"AP Psych."

"There's no way your teacher is asking a bunch of schoolgirls to visit a prison."

"The cowards in my class are going to do it over the phone. But if I go in person, I'll get an automatic A. Please? My participation grade sucks."

Ari did not have a history of saying no to PJ. He humored her. He knew that her life was incredibly boring. In fact, he had designed it that way. He routinely fed the Abosches reports about pedophile cults targeting girls in school uniforms. He egged on their preexisting paranoia and convinced them to keep PJ locked in the house. When Greta almost convinced Roman to buy PJ a car for her birthday, he reminded him of traffic fatality statistics, and then started going on about teen pregnancy.

When Ari was a child, his elementary school did a Kosher version of a marshmallow test with Hanukkah gelt. His teachers put a chocolate coin in front of each child and set a timer that rang every ten minutes for an hour. Every child that abstained from eating the gelt would get an additional coin for every ten minutes of resistance. Ari kept his chin parallel to the floor, fueled by the rustling of wrappers around the room. It made him smile. When the fifth alarm went off, Ari was the last student without a gluttonous chocolate stain around his lips. When the teacher announced the end of the experiment, he proudly collected the six gelt and offered one to the ugliest girl in the class, who had caved around the twenty-minute mark. He passed out the rest of his coins to every person in the room that he pitied, including his teacher.

PJ and Ari's affair barely registered to them as a secret. It felt more like a parallel reality or a quickly forgotten dream. The affair brought them no stress or moral anxiety. Neither of them had ever considered sharing it with anyone else, or even imagined it. They didn't have to fight urges or hold back from being publicly affectionate—in public, their relationship was chemically different. Blood dries brown, semen dries clear. Sebum turns black when exposed to oxygen. They never so much as hugged outside of Ari's house and hotel rooms. The lack of interference made their bond timeless. It was the most stable, comfortable relationship either of them would ever experience, a secret trapped in amber. *Purgatory is the real heaven*, Ari thought.

"Sometimes I get scared when I watch the footage with my dad, but I know he's watching me so I freeze my face like a statue."

"Scared of seeing someone die?"

"No, scared of becoming one of those crazy people on the street."

"That'll never happen to you. I'd never let that happen. You'd come live with me. Now that I think of it, I should get you hooked on crack. I should keep you here.

My plaything, he thought. *I created you. Your parents would have never gotten married without my intervention. You're mine.* "You can have as many prison boyfriends as you want but at the end of the day you're mine."

"I told you, it's for a school project," she teased.

He gawked at her from bed as she tried on a little blue dress. She had a stash of clothes she kept hidden at Ari's house. She couldn't even imagine how her father would react if he saw what his best friend was buying her. The dress barely covered her behind and the way she self-consciously tugged it down to her thigh gave her a charmingly vulnerable tic.

"This one. Flash him something while you're standing up. So quick he might think he hallucinated, but long enough for him to picture that exact shade of pink for the rest of his sorry days. He's going to become a psycho prison painter trying to chase that dragon. You'll drive all the dogs crazy at Powhatan Ridge. Lupine signed a contract with them last year. An experiment that has been going extremely well, actually. We take old retired German Shepherds that aged out of K9 units and have one per floor in the prison. Most inmates are terrified of dogs. Just *terrified*. They won't even *think* of someone the wrong way if they're in the same room as a dog. Mind you, half these dogs have little nubs for teeth and can barely walk up stairs. Getting contracts out of the Virginian prison system is as sweet as trying to get milk from your beautiful—"

With his mouth full, Ari finally stopped speaking for a brief moment. His lips warmed her skin and lulled her to sleep. He wrapped his large white cotton comforter around her shoulders and nestled into bed with her, enjoying her softly breathing on his chest, mumbling something in her sleep. He ran his finger along them and whispered back to her under his breath.

"Sixteen years ago, I introduced Roman to Greta, the best looking woman I knew. I understand

that time goes quickly. I can see time as clear as a map. I could have had Greta for myself, I

could have married her. But why marry her, when I could set her up with my best friend, and soon enough, have their daughter? The only thing better than Greta, is teenage Greta with half the

brains and ten times the ass. Roman made you for me."

*

PJ was granted a one hour visit in the Powhatan Ridge Correctional Center under the guise of being one of Ari's paralegals. Unfortunately, PJ had been staring at photos of Jason's face all night instead of looking up what a paralegal is supposed to be wearing, and she did go with the blue dress. Ari let her borrow an old black Suburban with a bench seat in the front. The leather smelled the way a sepia photograph looks. She didn't listen to music as she drove. She sat up straight and practiced what she would say to Cotton.

Jason was smaller than she expected, even though she had read his height and weight as recorded by the prison. She recognized the Illuminati pyramid floating over cotton plant clouds tattooed on his neck. She saw his arms for the first time, vascular and covered with their own encyclopedias of ink. He was handsome, with those Paul Newman downward canted eyes that make a good-looking man into a knee-weakening sensation. PJ brought a random stack of homework and started trying to look paralegalesque until she noticed the guards were only staring at her short skirt and cleavage.

"Journalist?"

"No." PJ leaned forward in her folding chair, whispering. "I just wanted to meet you."

"Case worker?"

"I'm a paralegal with Kharms & Roth," she said loudly for the guards to hear. "But I'm here on my own volition. I just think you're..." She trailed off, realizing how much fun she was having. Marveling that she could simply make a call and visit him, that he was always sitting right here in this prison waiting for her. That her visit was the most novel thing that could possibly happen to him that week.

"They told me you put money in my account. Thanks, I guess? What's your angle here though? Blackmail? I never touched you. I have the best alibi in the world. They said I have to talk to you for a full hour."

Jason only seemed to speak full sentences when he was being combative or paranoid. Other times, he slouched and slurred and making conversation with him was like paddling through a low river.

"You can buy a lot of those little oatmeal cakes for three hundred."

He looked down at the formica and tried to hide that she had deeply embarrassed him. "I don't buy those."

"What do you use your commissary for?"

Jason shrugged.

"Do you have a girlfriend waiting for you?"

He tried to hide his laugh. The inmate-chaser women who visited the prison were all the same. He had never seen one so young before. They tended to be big women with sexy, practiced voices. Bossy and obsessed with marionetting the lives of others. Zero self-control when it comes to sex and food. Lots of hair, sometimes fake glasses. Leopard print or cartoon earrings. "Fun" tights. Sometimes the hair was curly. Often, it was red. He looked into the future and tried to imagine life with this creature in front of him. Yes, PJ was not the first good-looking woman to come visit him under dubious circumstances. She looked good in her short light blue wrap dress that tied around her waist, cutting a line above her hip. She sat with her legs crossed and her huge thighs looked nice and cold, like the skin of a dead dolphin. He had seen this particular dress on a billboard once. Except in the advert, the dress was beige, and worn by a skinny brunette who could use a little cleanup on aisle Brow. The brunette looked barely over seventeen and posed with her back bent unnaturally, more like a slave than a ballerina. The billboards got taken down when PTA moms waged war against the hedonistic CEO of the clothing company. They replaced the billboards with pictures of girls' feet in the air, held up in the sky like clouds in white scrunchy socks. The new ads were somehow just as erotic.

"You know what PJ stands for? Not *Priscilla Joan, Polly Jean, Paulleen Jacque-leen* or something stupid and basic like that. It stands for *Perfect Judge*."

"Are you Mormon or something?"

"No, why."

"They name their kids stuff like that. What's your brother's name?"

"Don't have one."

"Good."

"Why is that good?" she asked, ready to be mad. Jason was threatened with the lie that Father Abosch was going to be listening to an HD recording of this chat between his daughter and her prison pen pal, if it wasn't already being broadcast live to a room full of bodyguards. He had been warned via a brief and curt phone conversation with Ari Roth.

"I'm an only child too."

She scooted back into the coarse plastic chair, relaxing her stomach, uncrossing her shaved legs in his line of sight. "Do you have friends in here?"

"I don't like talking about life in here."

"I saw the video of you getting arrested. It took me a while to find it. Some of your records have you under Anthony Cotton."

"Jason's my middle name but I like it better."

"One of the policemen who detained you had disabled the sound on his body cam. You know that rattling noise it makes when they turn the camera on or off? It sounds like a cross between a Polaroid flash going off, a lawn mower starting, and a fly getting stuck in a drinking glass. Anyways, he wasn't supposed to turn that sound off. That god, awful sound." her lips curled up. He liked her chapped-up mouth. She had too many doll-like qualities, she needed some kind of friction. Besides, he could imagine that the corners of her mouth were that red because—

"You're getting out of jail."

"I'm in prison," he retorted, not having processed what she just said.

"I got strip-searched to come here, Cotton."

"I bet they had a great morning. Most people who come through here don't look like you."

"I bet it's huge," she whispered.

He rubbed his head. His smirk told her that she was right. She threw her head back laughing in a way that made her breasts bounce. He wondered if this was one of her moves. He was trying not to hate her. He was excited but confused and very paranoid.

"When am I *allegedly* getting out?"

"Your sentence was vacated and you're getting a settlement. A pretty good one. But my uncle Ari is your conservator, and you don't see a dime of it unless you follow our rules."

"Rules?"

"Yes. You're going to get out of jail and stay in a halfway house of my uncle's choosing. Then, you get a job. Then, you rent an apartment equidistant between your parole officer and my school. It doesn't have to be nice, I won't be living there. I'll stay at my parent's house until I graduate. I'm getting a note to skip field hockey for the rest of the year and you are going to pick me up after fifth period every single day at 1:55 PM. Once I graduate, we can discuss moving in together. You might have to pretend to be my landlord, or whatever. It's just the neck tattoos, you know? My dad won't like them. Says it reduces opportunity. I want to go into law enforcement, it being the family business and all, but my dad says I'm too smart for that. He doesn't think of what he does as criminology. He says he's an *inventor.* I don't think that's a real job title anymore. He doesn't understand the way his technology shaped culture. He's a brilliant man."

The women who visited him tended to either brag about themselves or read his sins back at him to see his reaction. Emotional vampires. Their bodies always reflected their devouring personalities. PJ was a very early case. She could get this phase out of the way and lead a good life. Beautiful blonde women built like cellos have a great chance at good lives. When they have bad lives, it's all the more pathetic. A part of him wondered if she was lying until he saw the second deposit in his commissary, even more than she had promised over the phone.

Six Virginia inmates, including Jason, were freed after it was found that their rights were violated through body camera tampering. The idea came to PJ when she found that his arrest was not filmed with Lupine technology. She started to wonder how many Virginia counties were still using an outdated competitor. She brought the idea to Roman, who was often intrigued and impressed by his daughter's intuition. Jason got a job in a steakhouse and rented an apartment on a direct bus line from PJ's school. To keep their tryst secret, she nixed the idea of him picking her up from school and opted to take the bus herself. This is what PJ told herself when she was overcome with nausea at the knowledge that Jason couldn't afford a car yet. After a while, she would only come over to slouch into his couch and complain about high school. She got sick of his air mattress on the floor. The only table in the apartment was the rickety one on the balcony that was barely big enough to fit an ashtray. Still, the all-girls academy had her so pent up that once her winter depression cleared away she went back daily. The warm months made Cotton nervous— PJ was graduating in May. He'd sooner leave town than move in with her.

Roman was busy trying to prove that time started shrinking around the mid 1700s. His evidence included the emancipation of slaves on both hemispheres (he believed the letters between Alexander and Lincoln were forged by Russian gentiles creating a slave narrative for themselves) and Pangaea. He absentmindedly signed anything PJ put in front of him and agreed to anything she asked. The earth's core was overheating and pushing continents further apart every year.

Jason blew his settlement on video games, kratom, weed, and clothes. The enigma had worn off. Inside the prison, he seemed mysterious, careful with his words. Outside, she noticed he was sullen, lazy, and had a sixth-grade vocabulary. He wore dirty clothes that reeked of booze to see his PO. When he eventually ghosted her and left town, PJ packed up for her first year of college, wondering if she'd meet someone more suitable. She had never dated an equal. She never had to worry, impress, or compete. She wondered if she had any embarrassing habits leftover from the anaerobic chamber that was Holt. What would the other students notice about her? How long was the drive from campus to the nearest prison? She slammed a suitcase full of clothes on the floor. She wouldn't make the same mistake twice. She wouldn't bring another one home. *They're not like me. They never will be.* She pictured her father in the basement, his good heart, afraid to see a rabid criminal get tased after the twentieth warning. She wished she could bring him to Jason's apartment and show him his grime, filth, and degeneracy. *This is what they're really like, Dad. Even when you give them the world on a silver platter. How can*

*they ever rehabilitate when they can't plan two minutes into the future?
They deserve everything they get.*

*

PJ's roommate told her a story about the dorm they lived in.
Apparently, students kill themselves on campus all the time. *Read
about it,* she mumbled, dozing off in her satin nightcap. PJ eagerly
looked it up. Corinne was right, four suicides in two years. The most
recent one had jumped off the parking garage down the street. She
couldn't sleep and walked around campus with a flashlight to find
the suicide memorials. Some of them had small wreaths, crosses, and
bouquets. There was no memorial by the parking garage. Suicide
prevention, human trafficking hotlines, and free abortion fliers
covered the nearby bus stop like locusts. She sat down on the curb
and looked up Jason Cotton. She had gotten out of the habit of
compulsively searching his name after a busy move-in week. There
were four new hits on A. Jason Cotton. Apparently, he had used his
settlement to finally buy a car. She knew this because three days prior,
he was detained for sleeping in a parking lot in North Carolina, and
after two minutes of resisting orders, was shot to death.

PJ started looking for the video.

Love in the Age of the Algorithm

Anthony Galluzzo

"Never double-text. Girls don't like that now," my friend explained to me.

"Why?" I asked.

"It means you're needy."

"What?"

No reply.

Double-texting broadly refers to sending several text messages to someone before they respond to any one of them. Even one or two text messages that aren't directly solicited might be perceived to violate the ever multiplying "boundaries" which mark off the stunted—permeable yet brittle—self in the age of the internet.

The irony here is that text communication as such is a non-intrusive and relatively impersonal form of abbreviated exchange already—a digital version of telegraphy and telegraphic communique—especially when compared to the telephone calls texting has replaced. The phone call is now a dreaded thing for most people under the age of 65. One Gen Z interlocutor told me she feared the phone call because "you have to constantly fill up the silences. You don't know where it will go. You can't control it."

You could always hang up, but that is an aggressive act, and one which reminds us that the phone call is still one step removed from face-to-face contact and its uncertainties. Although what the phone call still retains is the voice of the other; the human voice, besides expressing feeling of all kinds, can persuade and seduce us into situations and commitments good and bad.

Text messaging represents yet another remove and requires even less: a few seconds to tap a one or two- or three-word response, yet so many of us now experience this convenience as a burden. We might see in this feeling a kind of inchoate protest against the 24/7 availability enabled by the digital technosphere, even as so many simultaneously prefer texting and screens to human contact exactly because we want to control it.

The urge to control "it" is also the urge to control "ick": contact between human beings with all their icky mess and surprise. This existential germophobia reveals why the text message has supplanted the phone call, the human voice, and, by extension, presence itself. You can text back if you want and when you want—today, next week, or never. Although, in the last case, if you're the one on the other side of the digital ghost strike, this shadow simulation of human relations often feels like Vladimir and Estragon waiting for Godot: "tell him you saw us."

Is the silent treatment a social more, or is it social sadism? Will *you* pass the test? Many won't since this kind of calculated withdrawal might also incite angst or at least a repetitive drumbeat of texts: *hello? hello? I am here. I am here.*

The human desire for recognition is fundamental, as G.F.W Hegel understood, but, now, according to the terms and conditions of our catabolic, capitalist digital shit circus, to act on this desire can be an epic fail. I guess there really is no sexual relation. Or any relation whatsoever. Is it any wonder that attachment theory is having a boom when our digital dispensation is better described as an assembly line for the mass manufacture of anxious and avoidant attachment styles?

But shouldn't I at least celebrate all this writing as a downwardly mobile and perpetually disgruntled English teacher? Rather than ushering in some second great age of epistolary lit, text and social media communication have transformed written expression into "text speak" or post-literate code: minimalist strings of acronyms, words reduced to homophonic letters (Wut u doing?) and emojis. Here we can see Marshall McLuhan's media determinism in action as the kind of long, densely figurative, and rhetorically adroit language that defines writing as a reflective and expressive medium—i.e. literature— and by which the written word replicates, or even extends, the persuasive and seductive powers of the human voice is precluded by our thumb tapping twittering machines. (And to attempt texting in a literary way is to invite unread texts and unseen ridicule.) Finally, it is exactly the telegraphic qualities of text speak that make text messaging a notoriously bad medium for conveying subtext and tone. As most of us have experienced first-hand, texting is more accurately described as a medium of miscommunication.

Dating—that most intensive pursuit of human connection—has been thoroughly transformed by these new technological forms as they have transformed the humans who seek to connect with each other. Courtship has always involved rituals, etiquettes, and games but now it seems that's all there is.

Although I have been a year single since a long-term relationship came to a terrible end this past spring, I still find what passes for dating ritual and etiquette in our desiccated present to be inexplicable at best and abominable at worst. I do know that too many are miserable and lonely. Yet these same complaining people all participate in a game now almost wholly mediated by screens, social media platforms, and dating apps—a game that includes tacit prohibitions against "double texting, " among other pathological norms—in which any demonstration of interest or feeling, particularly early on, is a "red flag" (this game is notably permeated by the noxious jargon of pop therapy) since this points to need and needs.

We are, in the notable formulation of philosopher Alasdair McIntyre, "dependent rational animals" while the quest for companionship and love is, almost by definition, a quest for a more interdependent form of being together (nowadays pathologized as "codependency"). Against this, our common creaturely condition, we're instead all enjoined to emulate the callow frat boy or the slightly sociopathic player who never calls you back.

At least we can say we've achieved something like gender parity in this area as women join men in the widespread rejection of sentiment and "neediness," today embossed with invocations of self-care and going our own way (which does not portend well for the society, does it?). As you have probably guessed, the focus of this essay is heterosexual pairing of a monogamic stripe and its sorry state, as we can note in the all the recent talk of "heteropessimism."

Much has been written on the many ways that Tinder, Hinge, and the rest remake intimate life into a pernicious version of online shopping as they transform potential mates into so many collections of data points to be combined in the most algorithmically efficient fashion. Of course efficiency in this case consists in retaining the users who would dispense with the app if they were to succeed in finding significant others: why failure to mate is built into the architecture of these systems. But I believe these systems would fail in any case, even if designed with the best of intentions, since attraction, not to speak of love, has an irreducibly qualitative dimension.

Jean-Pierre Dupuy invokes the Ancient Greek myth of Amphitryon in this regard. Zeus desires Amphitryon's wife Alcmene; Zeus accordingly transforms himself into a perfect simulation of Amphitryon, yet Alcmene recognizes the Olympian imposter and rejects him. Dupuy concludes: "When one loves somebody, one does not love a list of characteristics, even were it to be sufficiently exhaustive to distinguish the person in question from everyone else. The most perfect simulation still fails to capture something, and it is this 'something' which is the essence of love, that poor word that says everything and explains nothing. I greatly fear that the spontaneous ontology of those who wish to be the makers or re-creators of the world knows nothing of the beings that inhabit it but lists of characteristics" (258-259). Dupuy—writing in 2007 on the ethics of nanotechnology and the transhumanist project—accurately predicts the data point ontology that undergirds the dating app and its anhedonic economies of matchmaking.

A little bit of technological determinism is in order here. While I am older and recall a time before the simulacrum of life in the digital hologram, this is certainly not the case with many of the people participating in the game. More used to interacting with social media avatars—trolling and blocking—we can now observe this virtual poison as it spreads through the flesh-and-blood, if algorithmically managed, social body. Which is why psycho-pathological tics out of the DSM-IV—like ghosting, splitting, and the kind of troll show performance that precludes any trace of vulnerability—are our new norms and imperatives.

This process arguably represents the last stage of the rationalization process described in different ways by Karl Marx and Max Weber or their followers. In the past, you met your dates, partners, and future life mates through those longstanding networks of extended family and friends that roughly correspond to the idea of Gemeinschaft ("community") as theorized in the German sociological tradition. It was exactly the primacy of communal ties, with their attendant obligations and consequences, that precluded behaviors like ghosting. You had to deal with your friend's sister or your brother-in-law's nephew if you wanted to split, or else. You couldn't just vanish.

With the shift into Gesellschaft ("society"), impersonal contractual relations—along the lines of wage labor, business transactions, and market calculations—increasingly colored all interpersonal connections, including intimate ones outside of the public sphere. In this story, internet dating and its swipe right "culture" of exchangeable shopping options are one reified end point of the capitalist modernization process and its colonization of the lifeworld.

While these ideal types are useful in deciphering long term historical and social transformations, this narrative is too simple. The marriage contract, for example, was for most of recorded history just that: an arrangement among families until the ideal of companionate marriage was adopted as a western norm during the modern period. And, as Marxist feminists like Silvia Federici argue, after the decline of the household economy, rather than a haven in a heartless world, the intimate sphere of women, children, hearth, and home is a reservoir of reproductive labor: the unpaid foundation for the paid work upon which capitalism depends. This is reductive of course—the bourgeois family can be many things at once, both good and bad—but a useful reminder, nonetheless.

Until the day before yesterday, romantic love had always existed in the interstices and among the shadows—passion arrayed against formal reproductive arrangements—as we can see in the medieval literature of courtly love with its focus on unrequited, idealized, and tacitly adulterous longing. The union of love in this sense and formal partnership arrangements that include children is a modern achievement—mostly a good one—in part attributable to romanticism, modernity's first counterculture. The virtualization and quantification of erotic life by way of digital prostheses represent a bad break with this more recent hybrid tradition.

Yet so much of our new ethos recalls the rake and the flirt in automated and algorithmic forms. And, as our perennialist critic might object, you only have to read Samuel Richardson or Jane Austen to know that libertinism and coquetry—very much aligned with letter writing and the epistolary novel at their high points—long predate the internet. Perhaps, but what was once exceptional—hence the stuff of novels—is now pervasive in a mechanically unconscious manner, as the dominant etiquette increasingly resembles a cluster b personality disorder.

The libertine ethos was always a quantitative one anyway, from Lord Rochester to the Marquis de Sade: the higher the body count the better, with bodies-conquests understood in blatantly material-mechanical terms and often accompanied by explicit commitments to the most reductive forms of materialism and/or rationalism. (Theodor Adorno and Max Horkheimer first recognized this kinship between a certain strand of enlightenment rationalism and Sade's libertinism in their *Dialectic of Enlightenment*.)

Coquetry similarly revels in successfully conquering and cultivating suitors, admirers, fans. String them along. Crush them. Record the wins in the journal-spreadsheet. Post the wins on your IG story or incorporate them into your OF routine. The game—which encompasses both internet instilled interpersonal mores and the algorithmic dating machines whereby the Sadean utopia of bodies as numbers and nothing but numbers are realized—represents an old dream of reason come to "life." We have arrived at something like a high-tech proof of concept!

Meanwhile—and with techno-material base and memetic superstructure in mind—is it any wonder that we today see an explosion of praise for transactional relationships on both the libertarian right and an ostensibly Marxist left? Ours is a zeitgeist both incoherent and ironic. Consider our frothing US right wingers who see "cultural Marxism" in the moralizing technocratic liberalism of the DP, while too many self-described, extremely online, American Marxists believe that the abolition of capitalist property relations are simply one utilitarian precondition for the realization of various self-interested enterprises. These enterprises are indistinguishable from libertarian visions of freedom (even as they are inconceivable outside the capitalist cash nexus—iPhones for everyone?) So much for the pursuit of a non-alienated life! And right, left, center are all of course equally techno-utopian.

As the most incisive technology critics—from Ivan Illich to Langdon Winner—have noted, social and technological determination are inextricable from each other. A big chunk of the same generational cohort that grew up in these various virtual worlds were simultaneously raised as so much human capital by helicopter parents who instilled in their offspring a neurotic fear of life and its messy contingencies; these tendencies were (and are) magnified by digital platforms that instill in their users the illusion of control (even as Facebook, Instagram, and the rest mine and manipulate them, mine and manipulate us).

We can, in other words, detect in the game playing that characterizes so much of our hypermediated dating—so much of our hypermediated interpersonal—lives a fear of life (and feeling). Hence "red flags" and the tacit hoops: tests animated by a delusional urge to immunize us against present and future failure, heartbreak, and loss.

But these things—and the possibility of failure—are exactly the point as Martin Hägglund contends: "Caring about someone or something requires that we believe in its value, but it also requires that we believe that what is valued can cease to be. In order to care, we believe in the future not only as a chance but also as a risk. Only in the light of risk—only in the light of possible failure or loss—can we be committed to sustaining the life of what we value" (10). It is within the horizon of finitude that any commitment has weight as you or I embrace the risk of committing to this person or that project, knowing such risky commitments could very well come to nothing or worse. Feeling powers such leaps of faith.

And what is this feeling? Love. The discourse on love is a long and complicated one. If we don't have love, it's all for nothing, right? St. Paul is correct but he's talking about another kind of love—charity, agape. I have come to believe that the different sorts of love —philia, eros, agape—are permeable, that these are overlapping magisteria.

When Socrates ventriloquizes the priestess Diotima in Plato's *Symposium*, Diotima offers us love as ladder: we move from erotic attachment to a particular person to love of all persons to love of all bodies, to love of all souls, to Love of Beauty and Truth as such. This is better, but it needn't be this hierarchical, nor so teleological. And there is no escape from embodiment.

Erotic attachment to particular bodies, which are ensouled, is incarnational gateway and end-in-itself. Eat the flesh, drink the blood: the best fucks are always sacramental. This is how we love the world and everyone in it. And this kind of attachment is shot through with the possibility of loss, and the thing itself.

Love is a complicated subject. Love deserves its own post, its own essay, its own books and bibles. Love makes us do crazy things. Love makes us break the law or at least shatter the canons of whatever counts as conventional wisdom (think Tristan, Isolde, Romeo, Juliet, Heathcliff, Cathy, think John Keats and Fanny Brawne, W.B. Yeats and Maude Gonne, Charles Merriweather and Caril-Anne Fugate, and on and on and on...).

"Whoever loves fulfills" and "transcends the law," to invoke the born-again Pharisee from Tarsus again. His words find a contemporary echo in pop chanteuse Lana Del Rey—one present day exemplar of a popular romantic tradition that includes Leonard Cohen and Prince, and which fuses holy and profane, undercutting the falsest of false dichotomies—or her lyrics as she marries erotic and religious registers through song:

> When all my friends say I should take some space
> Well, I can't envision that for a minute
> When I'm down on my knees, you're how I pray.

Love makes us throw everything away to move into a perpetually twilit sylvan world with the beloved one who made you feel alive again among the dark towers downstate. And then you both find more-than-life in that erotic epiphany and communion for what seems an eon until it all crashes and dies.

But, despite an unnamable pain that won't subside and a wound which doesn't heal... you don't regret any of it. You don't regret any one, any thing. The love you gained (then lost) recolored your gray life in shades of red and pink and blue like some prismatic marriage of bad bruise and aurora borealis. Here is the blood rainbow that will pass before your eyes when you die: something quantifiers, the algorithms they design, and the ersatz, "woke," moralizers who've aligned themselves with the new dispensation can never grasp.

After all this, perhaps one day you'll find yourself beside an other, damp with rain in a train station, sipping holiday themed concoctions and feeling it happen again. And if it did, it would be different—ecstatic and excruciating in its own manner—and maybe this time it would endure. Or maybe not. In which case, that one exquisitely beautiful and sublimely disastrous turn was your only shot. It is always worth the risk and certainly better than any assortative mating utility maximizing game under whose rules "double texting," that is, need, longing, and danger are all prohibited.

Too many present-day interpersonal pathologies emerge from a techno-prosthetic fear of commitment and its risks masked as a fantasy of control rooted in envy of our machines. Günther Anders notably theorized "Promethean shame" or the peculiarly modern desire to emulate our own high tech gadgets.

While our gadgets require service, they don't have needs after all. Our gadgets are rationally designed to achieve certain ends and our gadgets are virtually immortal, getting better and better with each new model and upgrade. Unlike their human designers: we are centaurs caught between our animal inheritance and the second natures—language, culture, and technology—that we've made and that also make us. We are tossed into the world, born bloody and screaming; we are fragile and imperfect creatures dependent on each other as social beings for so much despite any Frankensteinian fantasies of self-making; we grow old, we get sick, we die.

It's no wonder why the Frankensteins among us, the ones who dominate the culture through the digital technosphere, envy their gadgets or at least want to marry them (cf. The Singularity).

For Anders, this shame is one of hypermodernism's constitutive pathologies and it certainly animates the game. I earlier mentioned rakes and coquettes, and the way these overlapping forms of life have returned in tellingly bloodless and automated forms. Perhaps we might also discover the lineaments of a potential counter-culture—to be arrayed against the game and the larger algorithmic spectacle—

in another literary and philosophical movement from the (late) eighteenth and nineteenth centuries: romanticism. Surprise.

In the meantime, ditch the apps and the algorithms and their automated amatory Machiavellianism. Love them even when you lose them:

> Unwearied still, lover by lover,
> They paddle in the cold
> Companionable streams or climb the air;
> Their hearts have not grown old;
> Passion or conquest, wander where they will,
> Attend upon them still.
>
> But now they drift on the still water,
> Mysterious, beautiful;
> Among what rushes will they build,
> By what lake's edge or pool
> Delight men's eyes when I awake some day
> To find they have flown away?

Pirate Love

Nick Marotta

I'm with Pirate outside the START Recovery methadone clinic at the Myrtle-Broadway intersection in Bushwick trying to cop a bottle of methadone because I'm trying to quit dope hahaha. It's not going well. Pirate knows a lot of people there, it's his clinic, he goes every day except Sunday, and so we go up to loitering patients together, they like to hang outside there on Saturdays, some just to shoot the shit, some to sell their take-home bottles. Some people sold their dose because they were still doing dope. Pirate couldn't afford to go without his, he told me. To Pirate's surprise, the loitering methadone patients keep saying no when we ask for a bottle. One of them even warns us that we really need to be careful, and he points up to the train platform, a sort of concealed section, and says the cops are up there watching us, that they know who sells and buys bottles and that there would be retribution. It seems plausible to me but I don't really care. Pirate says that we probably came a little too late in the morning, everyone's already sold off their doses. We keep trying anyways, because I'm sure that I just need one bottle to wean myself off my habit at home, and then I'd jump off, maybe take some kratom to help, and be free of this shit. Plus I had done a shot that morning and it was a nice summer day, not too hot, so I didn't mind hanging around. Pirate keeps saying I don't know man, I don't know, it's not looking good, maybe come next Saturday. It had to be a Saturday because that's when people got take-home bottles, for Sunday. Pirate has given up hope for today, but I'm holding on.

Pirate is short, like 5'4" or 5'5", and stocky. A fifty-something light-skinned Puerto Rican guy who always wears some goofy lanyard around his neck holding his keys, he has one of those Bluetooth headsets that was popular in the aughts, and he has an eyepatch. He fell out once while he was too high and he was in a room with a big dog and the dog took him for dead and started munching on his face and tore out his eye. He showed me his hollowed-out socket once, it looked like shit. How I met Pirate was through this other guy, some fat junkie schlub who lived with his mother in Woodhaven, he was copping for me, middle-manning so I'd throw him enough money for a bag or two for himself, and one time he let me come along while he met up with this short old guy with an eyepatch, and I asked if I could get his number and he said sure and I said what do I call you and he said call me Pirate. I think his real name is Eric. Pirate also lives with his mother, but in Bushwick, three blocks from my place, and he's always good. So I see him every day and we became friends and when I told him I needed to quit he suggested I come with him Saturday morning to try to get a bottle so here we are, but I can't get a fucking bottle, fuck me.

I'm about to give up but then this tall young white guy with slicked back hair wearing long sleeves even though it's summer approaches me and asks me if I was looking for a bottle. I say yeah, you have one? And he says kinda fast yeah I got you it's gonna be 50. You got the money? Pirate intervenes then, he knows the guy, and he asks what's good, you got a bottle for my friend here? He says yeah yeah I just need a minute, I gotta go grab it. And then he starts doing some weird little dance, bopping his head and fists to the beat of some invisible music. Pirate asks him ain't you already been in there? I saw you in there. He stops dancing and says yeah yeah it's not my bottle I'm grabbing it from someone else hold on I gotta go call her, and then he walks away with his phone to his ear. Pirate eyes him walking off and then looks at me, his one eye squinting, and he says you can't trust that guy man, he's a crackhead, you can't trust him. Let's get outta here. And I say that guy smokes crack? Pirate says yeah man he's a fuckin crackhead you can't trust him. Let's go. I say nah, I wanna see what he says, I really need this bottle. Pirate says man you gotta listen to me, I know these people, you gotta listen. He's gonna try to fuck you. I say let's just see what he says. Pirate says man let's just come back next weekend. We both know you ain't gonna really quit anyways. I say nah man I'm quitting, I need this. Pirate sighs and throws up his hands and walks away to go to talk to someone else standing around outside the methadone clinic.

So I'm standing around by myself then, trying to keep an eye on this guy who said he'd get me a bottle, I don't even know his name, he's hanging out by a shitty little car with someone in the driver's seat, he puts his head through the window, maybe he's grabbing the bottle for me oh man I hope so. I realized that there was a very good chance this guy was trying to rip me off, but I figured there was no harm in seeing if he'd actually come through, that I'd know in the crucial moment whether he was actually ripping me off or not, and that I wouldn't let it happen, I wouldn't give him the money. I had a bad habit of being too optimistic with this kind of shit though. I had been beat way too many times to count. Partially because I was an easy mark, some scrawny very untough looking white kid from the suburbs, but also because I was too fucking optimistic. Like that night I was drunk and got off the subway and some poor fuck holding a food container asked me for a dollar and I asked him if he knew where to get some dog food and he said yeah I can get it how much you need and I said five bags and then I quickly said I'll give you 60 so you can get one for yourself and he said ok give me the money it's just a couple blocks away I'll be right back. This is the oldest fucking trick, the one everyone knows about, the give-me-the-money-I'll-be-right-back shit and of course you never see the motherfucker again. And I knew that, even drunk and stupid and craving a shot, I knew it was no good, I had already learned the hard way about this tactic, but instead of just walking away and waiting to cop from Pirate in the morning I said can I come with you? He said no my guy won't be happy. I said you're not trying to rip me off right? He looked offended and said no, here you can hold my food until I get back. He handed me the container. I opened it. He was offering some yellow rice and a couple pieces of chicken and iceberg lettuce as collateral. That was good enough for me. I handed him the 60 dollars, watched him turn a corner, and I pretty much knew I'd never see him again, but I waited a good 20, 30 minutes, I kept walking up and down the block hoping I'd see him, peeking around the corner he turned at, my optimism getting the better of me, thinking to myself, would he really give up this halal rice like that? I saw the guy a week or two later panhandling at the same stop, and I smirked at him when he asked me for a dollar and I said some shit like you never came back. I think he recognized me but he just said I don't know what you're talking about and I laughed and muttered whatever man as I walked away.

I'm daydreaming about all this shit when the guy I'm waiting on suddenly shouts yo come here, beckoning me, waving his hand. He starts dancing again as I walk over. When I get there he points one of his dancing hands at the person in the driver's seat, some woman with a ponytail and scabs on her face wearing a hoodie and staring straight ahead, not looking at me, and he says alright man I got a bottle for you from my friend here. Gimme the money and I'll hand it over. I say lemme see the bottle first. He groans and says fine man, Jesus you're paranoid, and he pulls something out of his pocket and he grips the entire thing so I can't really see it, but there's a cap, it looks like some kind of little bottle. I say I can't see it. He makes some annoyed mouth noise and says man we gotta do this quick, fuckin cops everywhere just gimme the money and take the bottle and get outta here. I say I want to see the bottle first. He mutters something under his breath and hands it to me. It's a small, clear medicinal bottle but the label is torn off and the liquid inside is completely transparent. I say this looks like water. He says it's meth man just take it. The crucial moment has arrived. I look at the bottle again. I don't really know what methadone even looks like, but I have a strong suspicion it doesn't look just like water. I hand the bottle back to him and say nah man, thanks anyways. I walk away and he calls me a bitch and I never see him again. On the walk back to our area, Pirate is yelling at me, telling me I fucking told you man, why don't you listen, I care about you man, why didn't you fucking listen to me?!?! I said I was sorry and he calmed down after a while, muttering you gotta fucking listen to me intermittently. Before we part ways, I buy a bundle from him. I shoot up as soon as I get home. It's fire and I text Pirate, this shit is fire, you're my best friend, and he texts back you too bud, love you man, and I just lay back on my mattress, basking in that Pirate love.

Poems

Philip Traylen

Regarding the crucifixion

Long poems seem to be popular these days. I'm not sure
why—there isn't anything to say. Certainly there are many
things—but how can you know
whether they want to be described? You can't
interview a bush or a spanner, and yet
isn't that what poets, at least the good ones,
are trying to do? On the other hand,
isn't it easier, and perhaps better,
to use a hammer to fix a nail to a wall
or a wrist to a cross
than to say what that hammer, or that nail
or even that slender wrist
'is', or what it's doing? Yes, what *are* your hands doing
nailed to that tall cross? It's not for me to say, I get that,
but you're hardly qualified either;
we now know—'psychologists have demonstrated'—
that people's sense of what they're up to
is typically way off. You have to wait a couple of thousand
years before the true meaning of your
activities takes shape. But you had
other ideas—that's why you were hanging up there
in the first place.

For Will Smith

"Take your wife's name out
of your *own* mouth, for once.
Take it out and let me inspect it.
I need to know what you're
up to in there." Okay,
I said, and began the arduous
process. But I was thinking
of something else: Spring,
the complete rejuvenation
of nature from eternal
death. I didn't mention this
then, and I'm not going to mention it now;
one must have something
in reserve, as my mother said,
and if that something
is the immediate concrete
resurrection of all life
so much the better. Anyway,
you have to make do with what you have.

Strange Young Girls

Ella Schmidt

I. The Married Girl

The voice was pale and unsure of itself—this was the nerve center of its beauty, the falter before it found its stride. A girl's voice, one that held no particular emotion, though a few of us looked up from our phones in suspicion, prepared to be accosted in some way. She didn't command much attention from the subway car, didn't even seek to catch the eye of another passenger. Instead, she kept her gaze low and delivered what seemed to be a brief sermon. The train paused in the station as if to hear her out. She informed us that God would not let anyone die outside His love, invited us to forgo our selfish interests for a while and give some thought to the state of our souls. And that was all. She offered no literature, extolled no guru. When she finished, there was a palpable easing of tension, the thaw of our hardened layers of skepticism.

It was a delicate intervention. Before the girl talked about God, I'd devoted my commute to getting worked up about how the men Hiroyuki calls my "pedophile boyfriends" are better public intellectuals than I am—making me an obvious muse, making me stupid. This was a vain and pointless line of thought, and the girl's interruption came with the kind of exquisite timing that makes a person give God a second thought. With each stop, the shuffling of passengers in and out left the girl's audience altered and dispersed,

73

though she never repeated herself for the newcomers, who went about their commutes with no knowledge of the passive evangelizing that preceded this quiet.

Those who witnessed the girl's soft proselytizing had lived different, less coherent lives than those who got on after us. It was late; I was alone and losing the feeling I'd spent all night inventing at the bar, perfect-hypnotic-drunk. I missed my stop, and missed another before the lapse caught up to me. Because I am often getting on and off trains at the wrong places or in the wrong ways, I've developed an outsized reaction to the error: first I think I'm lost, and then that I am the wrong kind of person for the world, incompetent to get where I need to go.

Maybe it was because I wasn't dressed for the wet snow coming up—I was wearing tights and miu miu ballet heels I got on eBay in my efforts to become a beautiful idiot—or maybe it was because the girl's sermon reminded me of her that I rode to Alice's stop.

The strange young girl—the one walking the strip, hiding her madness, sweet soft and placid in the old song—is an obvious muse. More obvious than the washed-up old scholar writing his obituary on his phone in bed beside her, and more interesting. The obvious muse doesn't seem to know why she sleeps where she sleeps, or with what people. Assign reason and order to her, but it won't lay flat. Alice got married two years ago, when we left college. I expressed no opinion, gave no objection; I'm happy for you, I said again and again—until it didn't sound so strained; until I meant it.

This is the story of one night with Alice: she opens the door in her *I Beat Anorexia* t-shirt and doesn't pretend to be glad to see me.

"God," she says. "You're not dressed for the weather."

"I tried calling."

"No you didn't."

"You're drunk."

"Ella, that's what you say when *you're* drunk."

Alice has a nice place, nicer than a girl is supposed to have at our age. A two-bedroom whose sterile, renovated insides resist the decay and genuine beauty lining her street. I live with a 65-year-old Japanese DJ who lets me stay in his spare room for a thousand bucks a month. He waits up for me when I'm out, unless it is very cold, because according to Hiroyuki "rapists don't go out in the cold." Sometimes, I like to imagine we've gotten ourselves fixed in a tense, dire romance that neither of us can act upon. Other times I like to imagine he is my surrogate father. We live in that part of Bushwick where the J and M trains clatter overhead. I moved in with Hiroyuki because he was the first person who didn't run a background check or make me sign a lease. My credit score had just dipped below what any legitimate landlord, however desperate, would stoop to accept. Hiroyuki believes, like I do, that I will marry someone rich, ideally the bad-dad type who imparts financial literacy to his children and little else. Older than me. I like this fate. All my rich friends have cruel fathers, inattentive and withholding of love. They feel guilty for resenting them, because they are the same terrible men who gave them good credit scores and expensive educations. The rich have a peculiar gift for shame, for disowning the family name. I'd like to get them all in a room with their fathers, airing their grievances publicly, pawning the love they were given.

I was lucky: I was loved. I was loved so much, I had to sell my car to nudge my credit score above 550.

I present my theory to Alice. "Don't have sex with Hiroyuki," she says.

"Did I tell you he looked at some pictures of me online and said I wasn't always pretty?"

"You *weren't* always pretty," Alice says. "You used to be smart. Lie down with me. No, go rinse off first. There's a towel in the spare room."

"In the *spare room*," I mock.

When I'm clean and damp, she gives me a University of Missouri sweatshirt and flannel pajama pants.

"They'll be big on you."

"Not really."

"Yes, really. You're getting skinny. I don't know if it's because you're poor or anorexic or on drugs or what, but you're way too skinny. Don't smile, it's not a compliment. You look insane."

"Thanks," I say.

"Not a compliment."

"I meant thanks for the clothes."

"No you didn't."

I remember summers in Missouri, tornado sirens on the first of every month, baby oil in the sun on the decks of cul-de-sac swimming pools that the wealthy patrons of our babysitting careers owned but never used. I remember driving to the school tennis courts at night. She was so serious, even then, insisting between cigarettes that we should practice our serves. She might have been unhappy, but she knew what she needed to do to get where she was going. That was the first thing I envied about her.

The first time I saw Alice's naked body, I decided all girls should have tennis in their past.

I remember sleeping on the golf course at the country club and waking to the sprinklers passing over us before dawn. I remember competing for older guys, remember the lobsterman we both liked that time on vacation, remember him buying us Arbor Mist from the Circle K and ferrying us to the opposite shore, making sharp turns around the harbor at night just to hear us scream for him to stop, taking lashes of seaspray. I remember how fast and important everything was, and how new. I remember stealing birthstone rings from a kiosk at the mall. I remember getting on my knees in a prefab bathroom with the boy she loved. Strange young girls, biting each other's soft parts with our jealousy.

"Move over," Alice is saying. "You're on my hair."

"Let's play remember-when."

"I'm sleeping," she says.

"Remember," I ask in the dark, "when we were fifteen and sad we weren't old enough to vote for Hillary Clinton; remember we like *loved* Hillary Clinton?"

There is laughter as she recoils from our history. "What about the nights I had to babysit and you came over to copy my math homework," she says. "I remember spray tans before prom, how bad you were at tennis, mango juul pods."

I remember. And the dull hum of cicadas, and the stray cat she named ▯▯▯▯, Russian for *fluff* or *pubescence*, depending who you ask. I remember driving to college in New England, sleeping in Alice's car at truck stops.

"Remember," she continues, neither sleeping nor trying to sleep, "how I drove us to Kansas City so you could see that band manager, wasn't he like forty—you know you're still a bit like that, but now the men are older and worse—"

She sits up. Keeps going.

"I've been wanting to say, I mean—what are you doing around these post-ironic conservative types, they're just Nazis with art degrees, and they're making you stupid. You didn't used to be stupid. Don't you think it's embarrassing?"

I sit up. She keeps going.

"I'm serious. I remember when I liked you, before whatever this is, this residual love. You know what I think your problem is? Your problem is you go after these literary types twice your age or more, and by the time you realize they want to get married, you've moved on, and no one is happy, you're not happy—are you happy? You take too much klonopin and you're too skinny—don't smile. Your problem is they have nothing to give you and you have nothing to give them. They won't 'help'—"

She puts elaborate air quotes around "help." I get out of bed; she gets louder—

"—with your 'career'—"

I've walked away, but I can hear the air quotes—

"—they don't even think you're talented. Do you think they think you're talented? And don't those scene types all have sell-by dates, I mean. I mean you might focus on getting better or smarter, because it's over for you by 26. Wait, stop, come back, I'm sorry."

Alice follows me to the kitchen.

"It's just that people here don't know about beauty," she says. "They go to the kinds of art installations where someone is like *giving birth* in a kiddie pool. Or bars with girls reading bad poetry off their phones. You, reading bad poetry off your phone. And you're not allowed to talk, you're not allowed to laugh, you're not allowed to say anything except how *amazing* that was. That was *amazing*. You're always saying that."

"Do you have anything to drink?"

"I'm not drinking right now," says Alice.

"Stop."

Alice laughs, shakes her head: "It's not that. Just trying to be healthy."

"Why is everyone trying to be healthy all of a sudden. You used to puke into Dime Liquor bags over the side of the bed."

"That was you," Alice says.

"Maybe I'll get married," I threaten. "I'll wear press-on nails and a dress from Ultimate Bride and let him knock me up on a motel room floor in Nashville—don't laugh, I really will."

"Who would marry you? One of your pedophile boyfriends?"

"That's Hiroyuki's thing." I turn, flushed and defensive.

She sighs. "I really hope you don't sleep with Hiroyuki."

II. Pretty Baby

I sleep on the couch her husband brought in off the street six months ago. In the morning we're over it. I tell her the story of the girl's sermon on the train. I embellish a bit, adding a stabbing on the subway platform.

"I remember mega churches," I say. "I remember eating disorder camp. Remember that whole summer we were digging our nails into our mosquito bites. Putting our fingers down each other's throats in the woods."

"We were so mean to the bulimic girls," she smiles.

"Bulimics lack self-control," I remind her. "We gained like ten pounds between us that summer."

"Eleven pounds," Alice says. "I gained five and *you* gained six."

"I actually think you'd be a really good mom," I tell her. There is the impulse, always, to soften things.

"You just want to see me get fat," she says.

"Probably. Sorry."

"In seventh grade, you said I reminded you of a praying mantis."

"I was just jealous you were tall. I wanted to be a model but I was too short."

"Do you actually think being *short* was the only reason you couldn't be a model?"

"We'll never know," I say.

"You really are a narcissist, a little bit," she says.

"I think you have borderline personality disorder," I say.

"That's actually super misogynistic," says Alice. "Johnny hates your new friends too, by the way."

Alice and I have a joke we do ever since she got married. I say, *Are you still with that guy?* And she says, *Who, my husband?*

Then we laugh, in our rehearsed old way.

"Sometimes," I said to Hiroyuki on a late night we spent very drunk, how we like each other, "I think I shouldn't have had the abortion—sometimes I think I should have kept it, even just to look down at a baby, you know when they're little and they curl up on you, they look like cinnamon rolls, I mean they look so cute it just breaks you, I mean you want to literally eat them. Don't you think? I could have done it alone."

"No," Hiroyuki said. "You're really poor."

He tells me I'm depressed, as though my desire to die has hardened into something more earnest than everyone else's. I don't eat or sleep at the appropriate hours, he alleges; I don't have friends over; I'm out for entire weekends and in for entire weeks.

"You know what it really was?" I said to him. "I didn't want to get fat, get older. Who would want me like that, all stretched and scarred and loose, I mean I'd have like heavy tits, a bad waistline. Anyway, I'd be so jealous of the baby, all smug and perfect and clean. Don't laugh, you know what I'm talking about. It's all lovable and I'm all used up."

What I meant to say was: *Hiroyuki, what if I looked at it, just rinsed of my insides in the hospital sink, feeding and crying at comic intervals—what if I looked and realized I couldn't love it, couldn't tend to its survival, could only resent it, let it wail itself hoarse. What if I shook it. What if all I could think was: I used to be a babygirl. I used to get paid to be that kind of thing. I didn't like it but it got me out of some debt. And maybe I did like it, just a little—what if I liked it, and the baby took it from me.*

No, I imagine him saying; *you're being stupid.* Hiroyuki thinks I look stupid with makeup. He thinks I sound stupid when I talk about men. He thinks I am stupid when I wear short skirts. He thinks I couldn't place Japan on a map. ("Give me a map," I said. "I don't have one," he answered.)

But he does have a map: it's a map of New York City and it's pinned to a bulletin board in the kitchen. He makes grand, sweeping gestures when he describes the ethnic makeup of each neighborhood—these are Russians, he points; Jews over here, Dominicans there; where we are it used to be Japanese but now it's just anything.

A vague look comes over us, though we aren't looking at each other. He is distraught when he says *just anything.*

From *Eyes on Other Days*

Greg Gerke

A storm came into focus over the city, something characteristic of the cold mocking spring that had delivered itself only two weeks earlier. But it cut west at Stuyvesant High School and bore for Jersey City. The few drops fallen only activated the street garbage to shed odors it held while the cold had reigned.

They were sitting in the café with the cheapest products and the ugliest decor—something just above plywood encased by silver trim, chairs with cushions the color of vomit—things no single person could live amongst, things only an appeal-to-all edict from corporate could conjure.

He was her acquaintance, someone who knew her brother back in Tuscon. He'd been in the city for enough years to know how his ass fit in. He remembered her from the old subdivision. Blonde now, not taller but filled out, holding a glazed plumpness the city would shave off in a few months of running about after her destiny. Somewhere she'd meet a woman who would coax her into wearing other things, ensembles that didn't mark her as a member of a college team clique— if you wore black here, you wore black with etiquette, a black that went well with a sharp knife in hand, as the vamps from film noir. Women had pressure and presence then, now they had pecs. Still, she was luscious, mainly because of her Arizonian entablature. Her mind wasn't jagged with rent worries, or the specters of bedbugs or leering, toothless men on the subway. It was cylindrical and crypto-Buddhist with a splash of liberal leanings, rightly oxygenated; her arms still expected bannisters to support her wherever she walked—ha, welcome to hard times. The mind controlled the body, or so this half-handsome man, beveled with early eye lines, believed. He'd read it on his phone and some old idiot at a bar in Carroll Gardens told him as well. The old idiot probably wanted to sleep with him, but the husky man wilted after his advances were rebuffed, so his advice smelled true. His mind controlled his body, then, and his mind told him if he told her, You have beautiful eyes—and he would say it—she would loosen herself to him because of his positive vibe on top of the built-in trust of being her brother's friend. Even in this shitty café, they were making love already.

She smiled to give the impression of being impressed, but was she? Did she fool herself in his company? She was a little taken and the understories of her being pulled to please, for fear of the lonely life. What else did she have? A computer, a good winter coat. Back home, her often angry cat stewed. Mom said Fred wouldn't eat and then he attacked the flat screen when the Miss America was on, and she was like, What the hell, cat? I can't hold your hand through everything. You've got to get by on your own. It's not like you have to come up with a job and figure out the silly subway. You wake up, you get fed, and you get to look out the window for twelve hours, see the birdies, eat a fly, maybe dad crinkles up a piece of paper for you to bat around until you decide, This is stupid, old man. Jesus. I mean, I can't stress about these little things. My cat, Fred? He's not a part of my resumé. I don't want to work in a coffee shop—How can I help you today? No, like maybe grow your own coffee or at least grind it. Environmentalists holding their paper cups every morning. I can spell *thermos*, can they? Man, I've got to take it easy. He's cute—does he know he cut his neck shaving? And why did that guy in Union Square tell me the Beatle who wrote "All You Need is Love" and "Give Peace a Chance" was a wife-beater? Why do they have to be instigating? Keep your negativity local, everyone's fighting a hard battle.

This guy, he's probably just doing the best he can—what else can he do? One of millions. Am I smiling? Do I really mean my smile? Answer the question, you jerk.

Some blocks to the west in Hell's Kitchen, a man born in Florida sat under a scaffold hemming a ritzy apartment building. Cardboard, a rosé box broken down and folded, kept his body from the cold cement. A serge coat he'd found in a church basement covered him. He wouldn't have said *stolen*, but he didn't recount much anymore to living people. He knew the truth and no-one else not associated with his past needed to. His black boots were similarly gifted, but, hardly new so many months ago, they were now busted and the backs of his toes had been filed into a coarse, rope-like material from poking through and touching the city streets repeatedly. They also had fifty-cent-piece-sized holes in the arches. These breakdowns kept him from walking at times, but he'd long ago decided he'd walked enough—once going most of the way from the Mexican border to Monterey on foot. He couldn't catalogue his blue jeans or the sleeping bag smeared with road tar. It had warmed him through the winter and brought him to the doorstep of April. It had his smell or he had its—a question only for forensics.

His smell was wherever he was and he was his smell more than anything—a mixture of piss, pus, creosote, scalp, sperm, lint, pits, ass. All of which amounted to a cocktail served as his most complex and best feature—even a black bear would go bounding away from it. But his body was all he had. Long ago he'd curtailed the ache to bottle, label, and subsequently drink his pee. His body changed then, his mind too—self-sufficiency can fuck over man's humane impulses. But at least he respected life enough not to kill or kill himself. Sixty-some years and he could still breathe: not bothering to bitch, not cognizant enough to worry (except short prayers about weather); not loved, loving, or expected to love back. If truly beheld by citizens, they'd see all seasons in him, all that is mercurial and saturnine adding up to a zero point—unaccommodated man. Because his penis rose nightly, he averred he could produce, but it rose not at the unmasking of a body or intimacy with one he once liked to look at. It was a gradient of some miasma he couldn't conceive or at least a reaction against the cold, blood pooling to create another extension of warmth, or something representative of the urge to spray out what he drank— that of a regal diet preferring club soda over water, espresso over coffee.

The scaffold had a leak and he felt the side of his left leg getting unreasonably wet. He pulled himself up and swung over, cuddling the fat blue metal pipe though a large bolt bit into his rib cage— wetness always worse than pain.

Someone had been speaking to him for the last few minutes and he kept nodding his head in silence, opening his mouth in a stab at an answer, but surrounded as he was by a forest of silvery salty hair no-one could see it. For years, he hadn't either. Maybe his tongue had lost its color along with its musculature, moving from side to side like a slug he didn't recognize. Maybe—he couldn't feel it. The person had a high voice, but he believed it to be a man, though he hadn't looked closely. They were certainly talking to him about him, but what could he add as counter? The subject held no interest. He never asked for money, but sometimes he woke up showered in singles, fives, and the odd twenty. Most times there were bags of food, often leftovers from restaurants, specifically pastas with rich sauces from the neighborhood Italian establishments. It tasted the same, same as his mother made growing up. The same as two wives made—and even no better than the Safeway brands once tasted: stuff hardened, oversalted, and coagulated, that stuck to one's teeth, even if only ninety minutes from scratch.

The man who stood before him stopped talking and he knew he could look up because he could feel when someone's eyes left him. He was someone in uniform but not the ubiquitous doorman, rather someone who had other things to do, but stopped out of some feeling, not obligation. A great angst in those clean hands that wrung themselves.

He wished to be monkish in the face of kindness, but such sanctity could clog his rectum, which had recently begun working properly after a few harrowing years. He had nothing to say—weren't there monks like that? Anything the stranger could offer couldn't help the person who really needed help and a person with nothing can only give a lesson. He couldn't tell him that his caring was kind but misplaced—some monks would say that. Should he bring his palms together? The fresh-faced man required a sign or else he wouldn't leave—or worse, he'd call the City. He raised a hand and when the young man turned on his way from one of his fussy involutions, going at squirrel speed from phone to reality to phone and back, gesticulating to someone who couldn't see him, he saw the real hand and seemed to understand its deeper meanings, even the cautionary *Stop*. The young man soon said goodbye and the man's eyes cantered to the ground in reflex where a few dollars were held together by a paperclip.

At nine that same evening, on the top floor of a three-story brownstone on Henry Street in Brooklyn Heights, a forty-five-year-old woman finished her second high-impact session of ab exercises for the day. Her trunk had the same mottle as a crocodile's knobby head—most of the vessels, veins, and other lines wiring her stuck out so she resembled a part of the Bodies exhibit. If only she had been around in 1653 and Sir Thomas Browne had performed an anatomy lesson on her, much about the female propensity to adapt and go muscular might have been deciphered without the claptrap of a little over three hundred years of beauty registering as thick skin packed with fatty meat calories.

You're so cruelllll, she sang unaccompanied against the digital recording as she stepped in front of the bathroom mirror to inspect her bulbous front. Her 1500cc breast implants would never shrink even though her body had contracted at a rapid rate for the four years of her muscle fitness regimen on top of twelve more years of high aerobics, on top of four given to childbearing, on top of nine in high school track and field and collegiate swimming. After a supplement, she took a picture, but remembered she had already posted one after the first session on that glorious morning turned cruddy by what a Weather Channel flunky called the final whiskers of Old Man Winter. She didn't want any of her stalkers or former boyfriends on Fuckface to think she'd fallen too much in love with herself and what she could accomplish, how she could be forty-five with balloon breasts and possibly the best female abs in Brooklyn—not bad for a Seattle girl who married the right man and now had multiple bank accounts, each with well over seven figures. And what about those two sons? The second, Lane Jr., completing his first year at Harvard Business and the first, David Scott, working his way on the crew of the highest-rated contender for the America's Cup. Such a full life and with no body fat and no guilt the few days a week when she ate six squares of Godiva chocolate. She should reward herself for the new creature she had developed into—someone who might freeze menopause and create her own hormonal imbalance, one befitting a blonde woman's outrageous sex drive, rounded by a clitoris which might have been mistaken for a smallish male proboscis. Her husband could never hope to be enough to please, especially when he worked until after nine most nights, a practice their society took for granted. The man currently in stress at Deutsche Bank really only liked her for photo-ops and the gauche, expensive, sleeveless and backless, and belly-displaying dresses she wiggled around in for her shot at *cause célèbre*, the envy of all those poor old pumpkins he worked with. Her husband liked fine meats, rich cheeses, and richer desserts, and his beer gut had not nakedly met his wife's six pack since a few days after September 11th. Rubenesque secretaries at work were his speed, but golf had become more important than fucking, and making more and more money—nothing could break down that yen. Besides, the boys needed their parents to be together, to know mommy loved daddy and daddy loved mommy, and why not? They had invested so much money in them, while sheltering them from the world, shitty as it was for most everyone else. The word *spoiled* never crossed their palates' clefts, yet still they admitted the boys retained a childhood type of neediness.

She had her own network of people to absorb her nymphomania, including domineering orgasms, high-wire oral calisthenics (she did tongue yoga), and a penchant for playing the 5'7" Amazon—fuck the height, she had all else, and a husky voice, care of the 'roids, made to give orders. Young men, old men, African men, but a cop, a painter, and a neurologist were her main buddies currently. She had what she described as a love-like affinity for them all equally, although the painter knew best how to be aloof, hence wetting her the most.

Opening a bottle of mango Yin/Yang, the energy drink, she sat on their ten-thousand dollar couch and began to comb her fingernails over her abs in figure-eight motions, humming a new song by a British pop slut about being lifted by her beau to new all-world ecstasies. Then she scrolled through Fuckface, but nothing important had happened, just a plane crash in Mexico. She sang some more, then thought of her dead mother before cradling her abs. What would they do with the Big Sur house? Or the one in Barcelona? She didn't like how Spaniards looked at her—like it was her fault they felt the way they did about how her body was—her people were much better at hiding envy. A person has a right to be any way they want to be. That is what she'd learned over her years—you grasp life, you work hard, and there is success. The power to get anything. Hers was so full, look at her body and her boys. She touched herself and then brought out her pump, to make it bigger. Growing it felt so good. She turned on more music in her head and thought, If I videoed this, people would pay to see it.

During the mornings, Shawn heard the noises one hears all through life in the modern world, the world according to money and marketing. The kind babies started to become accustomed to in the 1920's and 1930's with the mass production and consumption of the automobile. These days, buildings went up in Brooklyn where smaller ones once stood because people needed places to live, and most of those people needed jobs, so why not keep building more to keep them employed. Trucks, transporting the heavy materials to build infrastructure, were always outfitted with great horns able to make a wren shit a white stream or command a squirrel to shoot to the top of the furthest tree available. The name Sunset Park sounded a lot nicer than it actually was. The eponymous park on the hill between 5th and 7th Avenues in the lower 40's stood out like a giant zit, though Shawn rarely visited because he lived twenty blocks and two avenues away. Sunset Park— it sounded like something out of San Francisco, and ten minutes from where he lived, he could find the wild waters of the Upper Bay off Owl's Head Park, a small hilly portion that gave a restricted view of that bay and the Brooklyn-Queens Expressway. The sadly underused docks there were best known to mostly Hispanic fisherman and frowning seagulls, just south of the enormously gated Army Terminal. The water could be gray like San Francisco, but it rarely had the fog. In the park, on land called Bay Ridge, there weren't so many trees and the ones standing weren't the gnarly, happy-to-be-alive trees one sees on the Left Coast, his birth coast—the planted planes were clipped and peeling, unsure of where to direct their branches because who knew now how the building codes would be flushed down the toilet to allow something ridiculous to stretch high, something that would have easily been rejected during the Reagan/Koch days. While the east side of Sunset stretched uphill to Fort Hamilton Parkway and had a predominantly Asian population, the Hispanic section, where Shawn lived, started around 5th Avenue and stretched all the way to the water. People here seemed happy enough. They ate empanadas, pupusas, and tacos, they played soccer, and they nonchalantly walked from the subway on 4th under the morass of the BQE's four-year construction project, with its abandoned trucks, cords of wood, and lengths of ribbed steel, to reach 2nd as if the mess were only one orange cone they had to avoid. Gentrification continued in the 40's and 50's, but he lived in the 60's—a white, and a recluse. Still, a few homes across the street had been sold over the winter and the construction that started on the ides of March was in full bloom two weeks later.

At 5:30 on this day, it was too early for construction noise just yet. Dogs, yes. For instance, the daily, sometimes pre-dawn walk of something he'd never seen, but what in aural form seemed like the manic episodes of the animated Tasmanian devil. Everyday, the owner (also unseen, but guessed to be retired, or a clueless but anal day worker) led Cujo-lite past a house containing its own asshole canine, and this set off the other, as behind that window was a woof—a tad muffled, but as operatic as Cujo-lite's incredible nervous breakdown. Sometimes they were set off in tandem, like an Olympian synchronized swim team, timing their barks to begin as close to unison as possible, and oftentimes dead on. And even if this mutt on high vanished and a retreating, bookish couple moved in and kept their shades drawn all day, Cujo-lite, negatively reinforced by the same route to pass in front of his foe, would still activate his howls in memorial. Then there was the next-door neighbor's blaring alarm clock. Because Shawn had been up one other weird morning, he found out it would actually start at 5:56, his cell time. It could be set wrong—it could register 5:55 or 6:00, but it went off in his world at 5:56 for some dippy reason, striking him through a closed window. Last summer, when he lived in the same apartment, he didn't hear it, so someone must have moved in or they didn't need to wake up so early then. But indeed they never did wake up or if they did, they liked the sound of the alarm because it would rarely end before seven-thirty, except for five-minute reprieves, a fact Shawn had a hard time believing possible, if more than one person lived in the three-unit structure, since he lived on the upper floor and apparently the neighbor's noise emitted from the first. He once made conversation with the alarmified's upstairs neighbor, a female stylist at Jeanne

D'Arc Hair, glossing the topic, and she looked at him like he had to be currently nuts. You can't hear anything? he repeated, shamefacedly. She looked at her shoes. It only occurred to him a few days later that she might have lied. Why would she want to aid him in bringing a complaint against a person who was ostensibly her landlord? This furthered his learning of how the world worked—even if his queries didn't begin there, sounds brought him to knowledge. But why? What knowledge? People lived by different codes. Hadn't he always known that? Sounds never bothered him in Oregon. Had he become a different person? He'd been on his morning subway commute when this hit, the N train teetering over the Manhattan Bridge, out from the bowels of the city, and he continued this thought until the el's of Queens by the East River, thirteen stops past where he should have exited, his straight mouth, dotted by bristles like young conifers, askew at his shirking of duty—he'd be more than forty minutes late. He turned the new translation of *The Idiot* closed over his thumb and nodded ingratiatingly to the open space before him, but in that space was a Chinese man who starkly stared him down. Shawn's joy of cognition extinguished when faced with something darkly concise in the person of an empurpled face with two violent eyes. Two idiots were in that seat and the man kept locked on them and Shawn silently begged him to leave him be, it was too early in the day to feel bad, inept, and maybe miserable.

When he circled back to the present, the alarm was absent, but somewhere a TV had come on—the piercing sonar of an old tube, looking in vain for a signal, indubitably and invisibly stratified toward every human brain in its immediate vicinity. He looked at the ceiling corner of his small room, half-expecting a security camera to be pointed at his bed or could it be a drone outside his window? His roommate next door, a fumbling man with a limp, given to silence even more than he, didn't have a TV, and he always slept late because he stayed up late. Could the signal be from the stylist next door? Though the properties were sheer with brick in between, could the signal shoot out her window and magically take a full U-turn into his? Or perhaps it originated across the street in a selfsame three-unit structure of beige brick, though that building had an owner that cared to refurbish the crumbling stone steps and avoid the USPS lawsuits that had enveloped Shawn's structure, leading to the mail being left near the broken front gate in a tall paint bucket with a plastic lid once lost and never replaced. Many months of sopping mail. But it didn't come from them, either.

Shawn curled his small second pillow under his right breast and pressed his hearing in as many directions as he could. Silence. A smile cracked his chapped lips. There was no TV. And there had never been one, at least not that he could hear. He existed though, as an overnight text message alerted him that today, though an ordinary Friday, was an Action day and people would be gathering at the Federal Courthouse at ten a.m. They needed him. They wanted him back, though he'd only come through once. He deleted it and tossed the phone into a mound of yesterday's clothes. Peeling back the cream-colored curtain revealed a sky that couldn't make up its mind.

He was a mildly angry thirty-eight, though nothing like Merrill. When he opened his door, he felt the wind of his roommate's before it shut. It didn't matter—the other man paid his rent and didn't bother him. Plus, he did his dishes or he made them and kept them in his room, where, unlike many loners, he often left his window wide open, even in January.

The toaster had been unplugged for some unforeseen reason, so Shawn plugged it in to darken his cheap bread. Often, he ran back to his room with his food, but today he remained in the ill-lit kitchen, examining his one remaining chicken pock on his left flank. He sat on a chair he'd found in Park Slope years ago, carrying it to where he then lived and celebrating the find with another roommate, a smiling girl who sometimes allowed him to sleep in her bed, though they didn't have actual sex—they cuddled sister-brother style, even mother-son style, or attractive second cousin with attracted second cousin style. He smiled and picked his nose.

Butter had been forgotten week after week and so he continued to use *Margarinalia*, a local artisanal brand that some kooky friend of Florence's had brought to his one dinner party in zip code 11220. The friend worked there and even tried to get Shawn to buy a *Margarinalia* T-shirt, sending a few emails over the next half-year, offering discounts at the store and adding invitations to see the man's band at some bars in Carroll Gardens. The substance spread unevenly; the knife, leaving a surface like a sledgehammer, had torn up the hard rye.

While chewing, he had an instinct to turn on a TV, a convenience he'd done well away from for a few years, though he had a computer, which offered an infinitude of media: articles, porn, subway fights, snuff and foreign films long unavailable (as well as *Talking to Strangers*, which according to Florence, was *the* most under-seen American narrative film of the 1980's), entire albums playing over *The Wizard of Oz* or any other cult film, Beethoven specials from Swedish television, cat videos, fail videos, bestiality, herpes message boards, wingnut websites, videos of how to build an oven, a yurt, a sauna, and a suitcase bomb; seventy years of most anything ever broadcast on American TV, including *Darkroom*—a horror series Shawn had nightmares from in the early eighties, after an episode showing the attack of toy army equipment on a real soldier. He'd searched for this once a few years ago and didn't find it—it existed on a downloading site for which he had the secret password from Florence, but it had been a momentary preoccupation. He'd seen the show at his grandmother's house in Portland. It had to have been a Saturday evening. His parents had shipped him off to have a rare night out, some affair requiring formal dress—there were photographs he studied long after in the family albums. Horrible flashes made the couple and others a ghostly entourage, sitting at a round banquet table in a hall doubling as a place to hold Sheepshead tournaments. His father's rectangular tie across a powder blue shirt. His mother in a dress cut to display her hips, some outfit he'd never see again. The camera often caught her expressions as they transitioned from timidity to embarrassment.

Again, a TV sound flickered. Definitely not a combo-tinnitus experience. Did it come from the courtyard? The roof? The downstairs neighbors did have a dish pointed at space. If the next-door neighbor left on her TV and it was 1982, the picture would eventually give out at the end of the day in the early morning hours, when there was no more programming or not enough that advertisers would take a chance on—funding didn't rule. Then the playing of the national anthem over stock patriotic photos before a soundless blank screen would appear at two or three, followed by the high tone accompanying a picture of color bars. The loud shrillness alerted someone asleep to switch over to the more comfortable bed. Maybe TVs were just always on now, akin to other electronica, especially security cameras recording every second with their fixed, panning, or droned frame.

Brushing the toast crumbs from his teeth, he thought of the reason he didn't create like his closest friends, Florence, the film critic, and Merrill, a Wallace Stevens scholar at work on a book about the dead man. A few years ago, it might have been will, but today it was passion-lacking—an elemental malady, but truly a teenage impasse. It explained why he had such friends. If he found people like himself what inspiration could be gained? How could he create if he sat thinking of useless things? Life had become drudgery. A job with the homeless that didn't stimulate him anymore. He had little energy to think of anything beyond getting through the day, except to read some Dostoevsky and vape when he got out of work. He didn't need a new outlet, a new love, a new town—he needed to remake his life. But it was just too hard. Not when he could sit and look through everything there ever was—and he didn't do that half as often as everyone else, freely forgetting his phone on occasion. But whenever he needed it, the internet complied.

He jumped over a puddle of oil scum under the BQE and twisted his body to fit through the space afforded between a giant air compressor and an I-beam jutting out from a stack the construction crew left abandoned since late January. A quicker way to his subway, though only by two minutes. In those two minutes, 9:00 and 9:01, Shawn's two email accounts received a combined thirty emails, half of which were asking him to buy something in some form, with two from Fuckface imploring him to rejoin the largest social media platform in history: Over two billion, "even the President will soon require everyone to have their own account, just like them," (they used *them* because the President was pan-gender, appealing to each). *Wouldn't you, Shawn Dessman, want to get thanked by the real President? Look at all you will be missing—Florence (yes, we know you really call her Flo-Jo or Florence, the Film Critic, from your past foray with us), Florence misses you—she can't share her awesome cinema articles with you because you are somewhere else, somewhere where the cool kids ain't. And what about Merrill? He's depressed again. Did you even know? Do you always have to be the last to get the important news? Come back. Come back and we'll squash that nasty rumor that you're a conceited cold fish. Come back and keep your nose out of the shame.*

In those two minutes, Shawn descended the rotting subway steps and said *No* to someone who asked for a swipe, then *No* again when he was asked again, adding that he used his swipe to get to work: I'm entering, he said, and the man said, So what? And Shawn looked at him, the condition of his shoes, how bloodshot the eyes, the dark teeth. He didn't have an answer and passed his hand out to the turnstiles where he swiped him in, assuring his being fifteen minutes late. The man didn't thank him.

I'll explain the problem in less than fifty words, she said into the phone. There are too many people who are working too much for too little pay and then there are too many people who are getting too much for the little that they do. It's simple. Simply fucked, though it looks good on paper.

Florence grabbed her hair and wrestled it back into a faux chignon, something drooping, improper, and windblown, unconsciously molding it after her arguments. Another person knocked at the door of the bathroom, but she ignored it, afraid to lose her train of ideas with a jobless friend who'd just been rejected by Trader Joe's.

I know films, but I watch people—all the time. When I walk through offices or am waiting on line somewhere. Most aren't doing work. They're on Fuckface or looking at things to buy or fantasy football. Or texting. Why is architecture so crummy, so shoddily built now—why does it take twice as long to build? The construction workers are looking at texts from their squeezes. *Don't forget to buy toilet paper, don't forget your son's birthday, don't forget to fuck me*. And to hell with class issues—the architects have the exact same texts. And so, they design grandma-tit-ugly buildings with no substance, no soul. They make more money, but they get the same texts. You think the dunderheads who built Chartres or Notre Dame were looking at distractions? Yeah, the sun and sky, but they thought about the work—that's why they're smarter and that's why I call them dunderheads, because I'm envious and striped enough to know they were stronger than us, than our collective hogshit ego, than the movie stars who pretend they are scientists or cultural anthropologists because they see a documentary. Those transiting up their wiggly ladders with stone to create—they *were* their work and were never better than it. Fuck the bicameral mind; they weren't savage. They were whole or wholer—we are the savages. We kill ten strangers because our wife left us—we drive two minutes to the post office, on our off day. We let the Wall Street fucks continually exploit us, so much so we'd kiss the gruel off their shoes if we thought they wouldn't be mad at us. Look at these kids—apologizing for everything, apologizing for farting so silently no one could hear it and then reacting to criticism by getting their teachers fired or suspended. Savage? Our egos are savage; eros is dead, and mimesis the only art. Florence plucked at her eyebrows. Hold on! There's a woman in here. She heard muffled complaints. *E ear oo quaking on own*.

Jesus Christ. You know how many toilets there are in this city? She opened the door and peered down at a squat white man in a security uniform. There's time limits on these restrooms, he said.

Oh, yeah? Did that come down from corporate? She wished she had chosen the higher heels to have made him seem more insignificant in the face of an overly tall woman who could call him cocksucker in four languages.

This is for the betterments of all our customers.

That's incorrect grammar. Betterment is a noun.

You know what I mean.

I know what you mean, but in a better world you'd know what you mean to say before opening your mouth.

He grunted and smiled like he also chewed a cork.

Bethany had stayed on the line and Florence rejoined her after kicking the store's insignia of a billygoat and pulling her underwear from her crack while heading to a screening.

There were days when the mirrors would talk back to her unending sass. They said, I've really had enough of you and how you always think you're going to put on lipstick and then change your mind, and by the by, why is outrage so riven in the lines of your face? Because of Nana Johannson, you have no debt. You have no man, but you have no debt. You get paid to write about movies, you get paid to watch them. You—not someone you want to be, but you. Why does your nose grouse like it's being forced to smell something it can't stomach? Why do your lips seem to bend inward like they are seemingly forever indisposed? What I'm getting at is the big one, the Pacific Ocean of questions. Have you chosen to be on this planet? Do you want to be here? Amongst friend and foe? Mostly foe—they want your job. Amidst another political scandal that will shake the foundations of our democracy? Amongst the robots who look away from faces every chance they can?

She had multiple answers for all these questions—she'd been in rehearsals for years. But for all the queries' truths, they were mere graffiti. One inquiry even went higher than the Pacific, dolphin in its delights, though coming and going like a shark's fin and then hiding in unexplained valves and kyles, concentrating her body into a Burma necessitating a dictatorial mind that would wag a finger if she flared a nostril in sleep. It so frightened her that when she saw it ghosting across her internal ticker tape, nothing trailed behind it, certainly not the sinuous mark of interrogation, or any other punctuation—a lapse that had her on-high copy editor steamed and shrieking because her thoughts weren't Sappho fragments, they didn't live like the garbage in texts, tweets, emails, and other ditsy digital errata; hers were as uniform as a barracks bed, as staunch as a bra from 1949, as ineffable as Stonehenge; if called on to shit, there would be nothing to wipe; they were that processed. But this one burglar lit up every few months, in places she'd never expect to see it, like when masturbating to Daniel Day Lewis's voice or ordering chilaquiles: Would she live *unwooed and unrespected fade*? What a line. When she searched it she found the number associated. She had fifteen years till the number of that sonnet, but she assumed she could lick it by then, because if she didn't, how could she go on? It was too easy to say men were scared of her. Some friend did mention it once and Florence tried not to buy a bat to break her legs. How could she cast such a caesura on her allure? It was even untrue. Some men did try, but falsity affixed to them. She could tell that a war between their projection of her and her annoyance at them would ensue—how can you be attracted to men who repel, who tell you everything they think they feel, making your beauty into the reason they will confess how wrongly they've treated women, but also how originally and wrongly their mothers treated them? Then all the hijinks of breastfeeding, potty-training, and the generally varicose mama's boy syndrome, most of which counted as bullshit because they made up memories about breasts—a child's mind is notoriously gooey and about as dependable as cheesecloth.

A gangly woman from New Jersey with white porcelain skin and golden Botticelli tresses, she couldn't locate her G spot, but she grokked film and emotion—she knew Alan Parker from Stephen Frears, a Rohmer from a Rivette, anamorphic from Cinemascope, pride from vanity, love from lust, loneliness from aloneness, amelioration from ingratiation, and jealousy from envy. When she needed attention she just lived—all she had to do was wake up and go out of her house. When she passed the bodega, they watched her. Her neck—long. Her hand—large. Her eyes occupied the opposite hemispheres of her face in imitation of some of the most repugnant reptiles and late 20th century female beauty. She never deigned, never curtseyed, barely bent, even if she had to pick up a bag of groceries. To cut into her mind's occupation, she walked a few days a week from Brooklyn to Manhattan over the cherished bridge and then, going north at City Hall Park, up Centre and into Lafayette, which led into fashionably shitty Soho, where people were so conceited they wouldn't look at anyone unless they wanted to kiss them, deferring to their phones when ordering food or accepting change. Eventually, she would fly to the plethora of screening rooms around Union Square. Years before, Merrill had impressed on her how many miles Wallace Stevens walked in his youth. Look at the good it did him, he told her, though without a before and after, how would she really know? She became used to walking and enjoyed the movement. She went through shoes like she sat in a mill, grinding off the soles, while her feet held many levels of blisters, so pictures of them could fill an entire book devoted to dermatologic vagaries. So what? It kept her legs young and probably helped the heart that asked to ache about how she chose who she could become intimate with. While her head bellowed for the effete, overly-intellectual men she wanted to get sexual with, the ventricles, arteries, atria, and aorta were getting an overabundance of oxygen, as they worried how the rugged mountain man was rebuked, again and again. She smoked pot only once a season, if that. Drugs, once something revered, were, as the Right always believed, for the weak—a sensational barrier against pain, misunderstanding, and the fact that factory orders were up .02% for the month of February in the US, something newsworthy on NPR.

The face she showed the world had been sculpted by Rodin, colored like a Bonnard, and written about by Rilke, in "[you who never arrived]." Florence lived every word of that uncollected and untitled poem each day her mind told her it was a new day. She rued duplicating the impatience replete on the faces of the mostly white people who lived near her in the Slope—really it was a blankness, which she could only describe as redolent of the apathetic, though card-carrying knee-jerk liberal, best burrito/brunch snobs who watched the same acclaimed TV shows (bullshit, her inner voice cried, TV was still the inferior art). She would never be caught staring at anything like a vista, only to uncouple via device to text a thought or take a picture—signatures more people were exposed to closer to the cradle, as parents looked at their screens with as much avidity and heartspersonship as they did their offspring. So, kids had to be given their own screens or they would be left out and made to feel that they weren't that interesting to their creators because they were looked at less and less. At least this way the kiddies would see what the fuss, what the fuck, and by golly look at the cartoon people, much more interesting than the dolts always looking at their phones.

Florence vied and stood for a more substantial enterprise—a stance more apt to spring into smile because it took less effort to rise from a non-crouched position. She could still be surprised by joy, by her fellow citizens. The little things that made them happy: giving a seat up for an older person on the subway, asking the breed of a stranger's dog (though they didn't ask a word about the stranger), or watching two people come together over a book both had read and the shared niceties of such an experience. A world existed to be seen, to be a witness to. She would rather display her reactions than file them away to be made into a bleak ironic anecdote for later consumption. Countering the culture, she reacted, and not with hidden rashes, welts, and warts. If someone littered, she balked and anger popped out a forehead vein. If a subway fight brewed, a more diplomatic, though cautious face took hold. If the odd gypsy sat on the street by Herald Square with a dirty-faced two-year-old in her lap (a scam...mostly, murmured homeless-outreach friend Shawn. The child is drugged to stay comatose for hours...I've talked to them, they aren't homeless, they have a place in Queens), sadness reigned and a burn behind both eyes started, signaling to her galleys there would be discharge. She might have hated humanity, but she liked people. In essence, she could fake the stance of a New Yorker, but inside was an animal who wouldn't laugh at an adult who took his or her teddy bear to bed. The individual, not the government, kept people going, kept them afloat. People's friends preserved, not the prospect of a new politician, a new law, or a sports team's winning ways—such window-dressing only divided and kept average folk incubating in disenchanting routines when they wanted so desperately to find "their own tribe." A newspaper for her father, TV for him and her friends—how time was spent as their days passed away like lozenges. And this throwing up of one's hands, this resignation—this is what she fought in her criticism. Narrative films should enjoin us to be better. Cinema was her life and it took real time to transcend, to see the world in a certain light. Film could never be merely a mirror like photography, because it moved as its duration engulfed. "Cinema is objective in time," as André Bazin wrote during the year the great war ended. Film played with our sense of self, it relegated and regulated—it magnified mistakes and showed how we look at each other, how we lie, how happiness begins in something as uncompromising as pond scum. The photographer in *Blow-Up* once had a certain popular weight, as Antonioni, by way of Cortazar, and through a strange compensatory ontology, chose him to be the initiated, to cast off the layers of shit that enclose the modern life, even in 1966. He's rich, he's a womanizer, but as the film proceeds, he is readying to give that up and, after accidentally photographing a murder in a park, he tells his agent, "Something fantastic's happened." When he's finally ready to get the body, he needs someone to come along, but he is at a party and everyone there is high. He can't break his fears and chooses to louse about, too. This was life, she teemed.

The great medium of propaganda, the silver screen, still generated billions worldwide. People still left their houses for the expansive image and, often, overcompensating sound, no matter if mostly for action, adventure, and thrills. Sometimes they still made good ones. Hopefully the one she sat down to would be, but then again...*A military veteran (Boss) leads a motley crew of ex-cons into the Saudi Arabian underworld in search of terrorists intent on attacking the New York Yankees.* She hoped the E.M. Nathanson estate would get a kickback. After a gag reflex following a first-minute beheading of someone resembling Babe Ruth, and then ten minutes of numbing incoherence, she started playing over the big screen with her small screen: *Blow-Up*'s park sequence with the photographer clandestinely taking the pictures. She could duplicate the shots, even some of their muted sounds—birds, wind in the trees, and clicks—and run through the roughly thirteen-minute sequence in real time (depending on if you included his time at the antique shop just before and after), thankfully obscuring the rest of the first act of *American Pastime Under Siege 2: Reggie's Reckoning*.

On September 7, 1923, Alfred A. Knopf published Wallace Stevens's first book, Harmonium, *just at the point of the great poet's departure on a cruise to Havana with his wife Elsa, the first extended trip in their then fourteen years of marriage. He is forty-three years old. He was forty-three years old.*

Fuck.

Merrill was forty-three years old. If it was his own monograph he wrote, he could say, *Merrill is forty-three years old*, but it would go in the bio. Maybe not. Authors didn't usually reveal their ages. He thought these things as he continued his work, his reason for being—a straightforward explication of Stevens with profound parts about the poetry, but a study grounded in the facts of the poet's life. He'd just reread the complete, though really "selected," letters, for the second time and he had enough grist to cast a new tale and fill it with the blustery thoughts he'd been accruing for four decades.

A fire truck blasted its way through the one-way street he lived on. Because it was the tail end of street cleaning, the driver of the FDNY truck had to go a little ballistic at the puzzle of ill-fitting cars sprinkled about. For fifteen minutes the loudest of all possible horns bellowed, ululating like a caged dragon not used to the cage, not used to not getting its way. It must have been Mrs. Finnegan's car. She couldn't hear, but even if she could, she wouldn't move it—not even if the NYPD put a gun to her head. She knew the former Mayor and even had some incriminating evidence on him—enough to scare a city—and because her nephew had obtained the rank of deputy editor at the *Times*, she was much more of a threat. Eventually, the putt-putt of a beeping reverse signal could be heard. She had won out, again. His parents never said a bad word about Mrs. Finnegan, though. They stressed diplomacy, especially in the case of neighbors.

He continued his sortilege. It was the introduction, so he could take it easy. Or was this the preface? Originally it had been Chapter One. The detail in "A Lot of People Bathing in a Stream." The line: *Good-fortuna of the grotesque, patroon*. Patroon—a-ha. Another of his delicious variations, this on an old Dutch word. Stevens liked to swim, so a scholar had said—a rather useless detail. Merrill didn't like to swim—did that mean he didn't like the poem? His book had to be ready for the committee at the University of Caledonia Press in three months. He had the outline, he had the main ideas, but he didn't have text, no actual sentences aside from the few he'd just written. Nine-thirty in the morning it was. Monday morning—the worst point of a writer's week.

An hour of dawdling. Then the main door to the apartment opened and closed swiftly. Wasn't she supposed to be with Marilyn until lunchtime? Nobody can perform a colonoscopy that fast. The voice said the voice's son's name.

Don't break my streak, he murmured. Don't, don't.

The voice continued, I need to talk to you.

Mom, I'm in the zone.

What zone?

Writing zone.

She opened his door. Just let me ask you—where are those free passes for the MoMA?

I don't have them.

But I gave them to you.

I gave them back.

Well, I don't have them and I want to take Marilyn there after her colonoscopy.

Why would someone want to go to the MoMA after a colonoscopy, wouldn't they want to go home and sit on a couch?

The Monet ends Wednesday.

Manet.

What?

It's not Monet, it's Manet.

Ends Wednesday. So where are the passes?

That's a question only you have the answer to.

So, I just walk in to bother you because at my age I've turned into a fooler, a trickster?

He turned from his writing desk. Mom, we have two levels of language going on. I'm giving you exacting answers. I gave the passes back to you a few weeks ago. You left Marilyn at the doctor's? What if something happened?

Oh, please. Why did you give the passes back to me?

Because I wouldn't be using them.

But that woman Helen set you up with...and it took her a lot of gall...she went out of her way...she took the bus across town to impress—

I didn't ask her to do that.

But Helen is so wonderful.

Merrill shook out his left wrist. Which Helen?

What?

Which Helen? Helen was setting me up with a woman called Helen. Named Helen also. Same. Similar. Fully the same.

His mother's jaw locked. Well, they're both wonderful, my God. What's wrong with Helen?

The Helen for me became sick. She's on antibiotics or something.

She waved at him. Oh, stop. Merrill. That's her playing. You have to break through that. It's a test.

She doesn't want to meet when she's sick. First impressions.

My God, Merrill, you can't fall for that. Helen told me Helen wanted to go to the MoMA with you.

We can go to the MoMA anytime.

No, you don't wait on-line with tourists on Friday afternoon. Like you're, like you're cattle. Behind those barricades. I know you. Not wanting to spend money.

It's fun to go on Fridays. All the interesting people.

You don't like people. You like quiet, you like parks with no people, airports with no people.

Hey, I'm a people person.

Like hell you are, Merrill. Didn't you see that Helen's picture? The smile. Recently divorced and smiling. That's a good sign—a positive sign. Thirty-six and she likes older men.

That's me.

It is you, but not for long. You have to get up. You have to strike.

Mom, you're talking like an infomercial.

I'm talking like your mother. You need romance. Not that Wallace Stevens and his ice cream poem every three seconds.

"The Emperor of Ice Cream."

Emperor whatever. It's just weird.

Maybe Helen will think I'm too weird, then.

Which Helen?

The one who'll be the mother of my children.

What?

The one who will have my dinner waiting for me when I come home.

Stop—you're always home. You'll cook for her. Read that cookbook I bought you. Now, where are the passes?

Merrill set his pen down. You know why I like talking to you?

Why?

Because we have zero communication. It's Sisyphean. We might as well be costumed and on stage.

We're always on stage.

He worked for another hour, fretting a semicolon, thinking the em dash better suited. Going to check Stevens's correspondence with poet Allen Tate led him to Tate's critical pieces on Stevens and he glossed them for nuggets, but the gloss turned into deep reading and Tate led him to R. P. Blackmur, the premiere New Critic, and Blackmur's infamous "Examples of Wallace Stevens," a piece no scholar would ever not know: "Another way of contrasting Mr. Stevens' kind of condensation with those of Eliot and Pound will emerge if we remember Mr. Stevens' *intentional* ambiguity." Why italicize "intentional"? Isn't the fact that he chose the word "intentional" enough to make it stand out, dare say even be intentional? These were the types of questions the committee would not have interest in. They wouldn't have read Blackmur and wouldn't care anymore, but still, they'd have to think his modern study competed against criticism some eighty years old, and at least have an epee poised to parry.

He stood up and puttered about in circles, trying to regenerate. Something seemed to strain in his belly. He looked down at it, hidden by fabric depicting a black and blue pattern of stripes, something woven in Venezuela—a gift from one of his mother's very well off friends all those years ago. Could the pain be connected to his stomach? Hard-boiled eggs always went down easily. When he had internal troubles they seemed to center on his inability to void or they had to do with his neck—an imaginary closing of the esophagus, an I-can't-breathe sensation like his collar was too tight, something brought on by a fear of falling or being pushed into a subway well. Fuck you then, subway; he had advances on his inheritance. And legs. It's just stress, Shawn told him, when Merrill wouldn't admit to the subway's churn with him. But what stress? He didn't have to do something he didn't like to do, or to pay rent because he didn't have any rent, but he carried the ignominy of living with his parents. Burning sludge he had to pussyfoot around every day in his mind and certainly many others'. His friends didn't live with mommy and daddy, most people twenty years younger than him didn't, but he remained in his own unique boat. To tell or not to tell? Remember that woman from Columbia? So, your mom told me you live at home with her? She said that? She did. I see. Now what? Now what, what? Now where do we go? Well, he said, you're still with me to get the explanation. Are you kidding me? You teach art history at Columbia, but you don't have anything better to do than eat Ethiopian and get an explanation? he said. I trusted your mom and thought her issue would be most promising. You trusted my mom because my father saved your father's life. That's a weird way of looking at it. Are you attracted to me? Physically, I mean. I mean, I'm balding, but I know that's been in style. I can't answer—I need the facts. You intellectualize beauty? Your mom said you liked Wallace Stevens. That I liked him? My dear, I don't just like Wallace Stevens. I'm not a zoo animal who prefers the feed bag.

So, he could be sensitive about it. Yet he didn't hide it on his internet profile. *Just a note: I do live with my parents. It is certainly a cost-cutting measure in these desperate times, but it's also about my belief in the ancient wisdom of the old tribes, where a son stayed close to the homestead, at work on his family's metaphoric escutcheon, even if the lineage isn't to be forwarded anytime soon.* He'd lived alone for some years. A decade in Harlem—don't ask. Going to NYU, fighting with faculty about how they should teach classes. He never called them out in public. It was always one on one—Excuse me, I just had a question about the last session. Merrill looked at the unfinished manuscript. Maybe he should become a librarian? But he saw what librarians did besides look at their Fuckface accounts and play video games. Just a week or two ago, a man went to the help desk at Lincoln Center's Performing Arts Library, where they only had books tied to the arts, and asked if they had books on furnaces. Then another requested a gun or at least a large knife to hurt someone who skipped the line for the computer.

From his desk drawer he took his nail clippers, a gift from his father. The father who never missed a day at the hospital, although the board had encouraged him to retire. He stayed on in an advisory role he extended back to full-time because, as he confessed to his son one night, Nobody knows what the hell they're doing. But he'd clipped his finger and toe nails yesterday. Shouldn't he keep his pen and notebook ready? It wasn't even noon. His mid-afternoon walk might be the best thing, but what would he do at three o'clock when he didn't feel inspired to exude lyric opinions? He couldn't take two walks; he didn't care for the throngs in Central Park that much. Trees and birds were nice, but people jogging with music blasting from their phones, or walking with them, head down, and bumping into him—save it.

On his desk, sitting in a corner, was his computer. He'd turned off the internet, except for reference sites, through a disabling program, until 4:30 pm—the end of his work day. It was 11:37. And for what, except for you, do I feel love? Did he speak to his computer or the woman inside it—the only part of the person he could access because she was still an email-only friend. Something heavy sagged from his mid-section and then instantly dropped away, like his second chakra had absorbed and then passed a hunk of happiness or an imaginary BM. He moved his wrist back and forth watching the creases become ridges of pink skin before flattening when he retroflexed the hand.

He'd been through breaking down the nearly irreversible internet shut-off system before, just a month prior. This time he seemed to know how to get it started, but because they were always improving or obfuscating, they made it harder for Merrill to regain access each time. First, he had to call the company's phone bank, then answer a series of security questions and take a short mandatory survey. Then they routed him to a branch office in Escondido for a brief interview about the reasons why he, Mr. Stein, wanted to override a requirement he'd painstakingly instituted only on January 1, and because this was the second time he'd asked to override, the interview portion became more chagrined, more challenging. This time, a woman with an Indian accent spoke with him: Mr. Stein, before we go through with this request, we want to make sure that we are helping you, our customer, to fully get 100% satisfaction. Because of your past history, I'll just ask, are you sure you want to do this?

Yes, of course I am. I'm of sound mind.

Of course, Mr. Stein. The issue is—what I'm getting at—it's like this—I can put through your request, we will override for today so you will have access early, but in the future, there will be consequences. And I mean the immediate future—instant future.

What do you mean? Why?

A deterrent against this happening. A penalty. A raising of rates.

Outrageous.

But effective. You now pay 69.95 a month for the service. Unfortunately, you will be going to 105.95 when I override you to get you back on the information superhighway before 4:30.

No one calls it that anymore. Wait, what   you said one-hundred?

105.95.

Are you human? This isn't in my contract.

It actually is—there is a clause about system overrides. We're also going to need to send a serviceman to your house—

But this is bullshit. It's all remote. I don't need a serviceman. And pay that fucking fee, too?

It's a one-time fee.

This is the only time I'm doing it. Of course it's one-time. What were you? A used car salesma-person?

The technician has to manually override your Apple. This is the new safeguard. It looks like we'll have a serviceman in your area around six tonight. That fee will be 49.95.

Well, golly. You know the internet turns on at 4:30.

Yes, so it seems. You might want to wait this one out.

The dating site was different from all others. That's why everyone wanted to be on it. That's why it was so good. You could only login from your own IP address—one device per customer—and they wouldn't let any numbers or emails pass until something substantial had been built, a minimum of three weeks. And it cost money per minute to use the system. He had to see what Olive might have said. For forty minutes he tried to think of a way around it and even found a small screwdriver before he saw there was no way to open his computer. Shawn was at work and Florence in a screening, but Florence seemed to be mad at him, or at least mad at something he represented. He hadn't seen her in a week, which could be construed as abnormal because he told her things he didn't tell Shawn, like the I-can't-breathe thing—she was the closest person to him. He didn't want it to always be secretive, but was, for the moment.

On the way to the park, he stopped at the used bookstore to see if Guy Davenport's Ezra Pound book had shown up. There weren't many copies in the world. The on-line retailers didn't have it and even the Columbia and NYU libraries had reported their copies lost or stolen. He might have to resort to the Library of Congress.

The bookstore owner had just changed the music from avant-garde classical to avant-garde jazz. The caddish fellow with a sloping salt and pepper Van Dyke turned from the counter, brusquely opening his newspaper. Merrill lowered his shoulder to obscure his profile as he passed the front desk, which held an old-fashioned cash register, a small confederate flag turned upside down, a bust of Bach, and a framed photo of George Orwell with a five-inch latitudinal cobweb, shading the steely unsmiling face. There had been more than one incident over the years, but the last had been the worst. He'd overhead the owner arguing lightly with someone about Ezra Pound and then the proud man wiped his slavishly looked after beard, massaging it with two fingers as pincers, and stated emphatically how Susan Sontag had personally told him Pound was shit and his reputation would soon go into the toilet. Merrill asked him if he'd ever read *Personae*, let alone *The Cantos*, but the owner ignored this. So Merrill said, I'm Jewish and I can vouch for Pound. His work, I mean. Don't give me that, the owner rebutted. Who cares if you're Jewish? My wife is Jewish. Do you want to go back to wearing a star on your sleeve?

Merrill looked at the other man, who seemed to bow out, then back to the owner. There's a great line of Henry James's that fits you like a wonder condom. Maybe you've read it because you've spent your life in a bookstore? It goes: *He is the same old sausage, fizzing and sputtering in his own grease*.

They had a first edition of the *Palm at the End of the Mind,* though it was scuffed with underlining on nearly ten pages. $40. A travesty. He peered down the way to see if the owner faced out or away and waited until it seemed the latter, but just as Merrill passed the register, the owner turned and frowned, ruffling his newspaper.

The flowers of spring: tulips, snowdrops and daffodils had poked themselves out of the murky sufficiently soaked earth and he walked along the bridle path into the Great Lawn, passing an onslaught of strollers, including one whose seated boy tried to whack Merrill's leg with a plastic hammer. The winds of April sent seeds and pollen across the grasses and into the air and he rubbed his eyes before cracking his pillbox filled with various medications. The hot dog vendor sold small bottles of water for six dollars. Who sets these prices? Merrill said, grudgingly handing over a ten. The Arabic man smiled and went to redistributing the dogs on the roller grill.

His regular bench had been taken by a man who shouted into his phone, It's fuckin'—what? It's fuckin'—shit. Fuckin' shame. I know. Don't tell me, I know. Merrill crossed east over the oval, where the midday sun lit up a stand of old oaks, and found another. He worked his tongue over his teeth to remove the pasty sensation of the three Benadryls. Then he sneezed.

Two young women in neon jogging suits walked by and one bent over to tie her shoe. They spoke of their boyfriends or husbands, actually one had one and the other had the other. The husband had committed himself to going golfing the weekend they were to drive to Cape Cod to see her parents. All he says are two words to me. Two words by way of excuse: It's Pebble Beach. Omg. It's Pebble Beach. Is that three?

They laughed and walked on. Merrill adjusted his sunglasses that fit over his real glasses. He hoped the woman from his dating site didn't talk like that. She couldn't, could she? Could someone who graduated Yale really speak in such a shrill tone? He hoped for someone not expectatory, but that wasn't even a word. In any case, it meant, by way of its root and his head: hectoring, smug, calling onto the carpet, everything done to them being an injustice, an inconvenience (*The gall of someone or something to do what I don't want them to do!*), everything a disappointment to their kingdom. Man-childs or woman-childs walking around with driver's licenses, healthy bank accounts, and other vague powers. In another ten years these types would rule the country. And if that was true, with all other advantages holding, it meant people from Yale could be expectatory, maybe more so.

They'd been corresponding for a few months. Apparently, Olive had become exhausted by her simple life in Boston and wouldn't continue to "see" people, only write like the women she looked up to, the great correspondents of years past: Madame de Sévigné, Dickinson, Colette, Woolf. *This is my letter to the world, who never wrote to me*, she prefaced last week's missive to him, quoting her cherished Emily, whose museum she visited every year at just this time. He wondered if Olive looked like Dickinson, full of librarian features: intense and irresolute face, bullish eyes, a wardrobe rich in ersatz fashions, a part in her hair. Olive hardly mentioned her physical body and, for a painful two seconds he imagined a very witty quadriplegic with the scent of sweet pee, but he shook out of that dastardly fear, no doubt concocted by his fumbling neurotica, his dark side—where the moon didn't shine, where the moon didn't even exist, where euthanasia and genocide were to be expected and never admonished, part and parcel of U.S. Foreign Policy. Ugh. A private woman, wasn't Olive? She kept a storehouse of thoughts shored up against the world. She had levels, depth (onion layers, he called them) redolent of some grand design; a woman paragoning description, hatched millennia prior, when surf and turf translated into sea world showmanship and people had to catch their own food. Quietly he continued to build her in his own fantasy, something that could be quite distant from the actual physical manifestation: imagining how the wind clipped her hair, how she ate sushi, and how she might be as photogenic as a ghoul. No, books made people beautiful.

And what about academia? Professors were getting suspended or fired every day for mouthing off on the internet or their phones. He couldn't picture her fitting that mold. Not only did she never script the hackneyed, *I like to curl up with a good book* line, she sometimes admitted her reading habits were haphazard, indulging in embarrassing page-turners to escape the grueling academic poseurs of the last century. Those details were fuzzy, and finally, unimportant. He needed to smell her, to find her twisting in liminal space, touching the same table he touched, speaking of something at the same moment, rallying the conversational ball, so it kept morphing in mid-air before it met the far person's metered mind.

He looked west to the Dakota and the sky beyond. "The Blue Buildings in the Summer Air." He tilted. *Go hunt for honey in his hair.* Merrill crossed his legs, satisfied but unable to accept the satisfaction his mind offered for three seconds by that line. It fled and he went back to worrying for three minutes. The frightening game would not let up, until Tex Message, as he called the phenomenon of all texts to him, came to the rescue. He checked and it had come from Florence: They've hit a home run with a terrorist's head. He knew a second one, the punchline, would soon follow and then the phone tolled: Where did I read the government just struck a distribution deal?

His sister—the sister he never had.

He walked south to the Belvedere Castle and the Delacorte Theater—Shakespeare in the Park, where some early preparations for the season began. A black saxophone player had set up at the base of the steps leading to the old castle—what castle could ever be called new? His sunglasses reflected the mostly tourists (mostly

German), who laid dollar bills into his velvet hat. Merrill stopped and listened to the tune reminiscent of the hey-day of jazz—'55? '58? But what did he know? A plaintive jingle, *de Profundis*, a moribund love song, strange in its filaments, though suggesting hope. A blubbering melody Merrill mainly heard, but it told of true experience. How a relationship had been forged through the pull of music.

A woman would see the man playing and she'd be taken by what he could make, what came from himself, but only came to focus outside of himself in something communicably manifest. He could be broke, but his soul was rich and she knew, with no family left—maybe a sister across the country, only a man's soul could take care of her. He slept wherever he could, but he had lived so hard, gleaning from the thousands he'd talked to in his journeys. She wanted streetsmarts, she wanted a life much less ordinary. They were the most unlikely couple until they started talking and they found out they made each other laugh—an essential in seduction. Then weeks of ecstasy. He'd lucked into a housesit and they could be together most of the day until he'd go practice and she would walk to the beach and read or write letters. Performance at night. Always different, something new. Could she tell this wouldn't always go on? The money would run out, the time would pass away, maybe even the romance would be the first to go. Most everything she told herself turned into the opposite, and soon, without any acknowledgement that he could feel this to be the truth. His decision to play the unattached, the unwilling anti-hero, who seems to hang upon the fringes, had come from the era of the jazz he played. Deep down, he couldn't realize his conscience would always exonerate his culpability. She is this beautiful, fragile flower that he will ultimately stomp. Like his forebears, he leaves her before she is ready to be let go of, certainly before he is. Never say goodbye, so the only images remaining are the good ones, but regret overlays it all.

The man took a winding way to end, the notes afraid to stop, but they did. Merrill clapped on instinct but he was the only one. Four other people nearby had been videoing the musician, but they stopped and sulked away.

Later, at 4:31, Merrill opened his inbox to find a message from Olive saying she would be coming to New York next week and would he like to meet her. He couldn't believe his luck and chalked it up to waiting out the internetless day. Patience, the virtue that enables dreams to come true. Happily, he ate his mother's cod and even joked about the Manet exhibition with her.

Poems

Matthew Gasda

Hamptons Bays

This is the last difficult memory before History was
over and the delicate hands of your voice folded into the
refusal of speech. An indifferent mode: the figural and immense
lost of knowing is forgotten, waved away into the realm of
appearances. I struggle to make sense of: your fractured
courage, your unbalanced mind. By appealing to reason
I've gotten nowhere.

Greenpoint Dive

You come around haltingly to what you mean: Latin swells over
the threshold of wanting more. Every moment drags itself out,
like a soldier clutching at the location of a wound. This nonsense
phrase indicates where consciousness is embedded with despair.
A new salvation: the vatic enterprise of pleasing the Blakean,
innocent, and wholly animal self: a rejection of duality. The
Vestal innocent sits on the lip of the tub, combing her hair.
She is before you as she always was.

Greyhound

Nicky von Hartz Shapiro

EXTERIOR. Late afternoon, approaching twilight. Winter. A high-pitched, screeching score accompanies a dark screen for several seconds. The sound carries into to an establishing shot of a large, two-story house. It's shingled with dark wood and draped with thick ivy branches. Snow dusts the ground. A light shines out from a large second-floor window.

From a continuous low angle, the camera slowly moves towards the front door of the house. It bobs slightly, the handheld look giving the impression that someone—or something—approaches. The shot lasts for at least a minute. The sound, coupled with the long duration of the shot, becomes uncomfortable.

The score abruptly stops with a cut to a young WOMAN, alone in the house. She clears a long, ovular dining table of the plate she's just eaten off, and carries the plate to the nearby kitchen. As she washes items in the sink, the camera slowly shifts to reveal the scene in the front yard, visible a few inches over her shoulder through a large corner window—the same window lit up in the opening shot. The barely perceptible, blurred outline of a dark, masked FIGURE looms before the gate overlooking the house. He approaches at a speed matching the slow opening pace of the camera. The scene remains silent other than the light clanking of plates in the sink.

A shrill bark interrupts the fragile serenity of the morning.

Fucking dog,

he thinks, dreary eyes blinking open, the vague outline of whooshing highway and whirring fields, set behind a dusty window cracked an inch to let in the cool air, on his left, the mushy figure of a lumpy woman, folded many times over, to his right. Both new, the fields and the woman; last time his eyes were open, the land had been full of trees, big, sharp branches, random bursts of pink, and the seat next to him had been open. How had she slid next to him without waking him up? What time is it? Where is he?

INTERIOR. Cut to WOMAN in front of a sink, flossing. She's shot through a mirror, at an angle which reveals the open door and hallway behind her. The scene remains silent but for the clicking of floss. Her meticulous pace, one tooth at a time, is suddenly interrupted. She notices something on her index finger; a close-up reveals a single drop of blood pooled there like a teardrop. Irritated, she turns on the sink, which flows loudly, to rinse both her finger and the dangling floss. This action triggers a cut framing a close-up of the rectangular sink. The sound of its running water is emphasized. A small pink dribble circles the drain and disappears. WOMAN switches off the bathroom light.

The bark of a dog, traveling from near the front of the bus, again cuts through the rattle.

Fucking dog,

he repeats in his mind. This time he turns to his right, rolls his eyes close enough to the direction of the shape next to him so that she might see but vaguely enough as to pass for coincidence. Even before pulling this little stunt, plausible deniability was something he thought about often.

Who brings a dog on a Greyhound? What kind of per—are dogs even allow—

He begins muttering silently to himself, furiously moving his lips around the contours of what might pass for legibility, lifting his gaze gently to determine if anyone around notices his eloquent nothings. The new woman's slumbrous eyelids droop, settling into an ambiguous position; maybe she's asleep, maybe not. A man with thick purple veins popping from his temples rests against the window across the aisle, staring aimlessly at a left hand draped in a dark tattoo of a trident, handle extending up his forearm, spikes winding down his three middle fingers. A freckled child in the aisle plays a video game on an oversized screen. The man's eyes flutter closed again. A glowing stencil, the exact, bright outline of the window-framed plains he'd been staring into just before, sears into the depths of his eyelids. The image tilts slightly to the right; soft, unidentifiable colors, hybrids of actual hues which his covered eyes strain to recreate, whorl imperceptibly across the dark vista.

MAN in glass box. Size: small bedroom. Fluorescent. Space outside dark, impression box suspended. Small, fuzzy dog appears, toy in mouth. MAN reaches for toy. Dog holds. MAN pulls harder. Dog snarls. Clenched jaws. MAN yanks harder. Dog grips harder. Teeth. Growls. MAN thinks. MAN smiles. Menacing. MAN grabs toy, pulls towards ceiling. Short legs lift. MAN raises dog higher by toy. Dog hangs. MAN, dog remain, several seconds, eye level. MAN, abrupt, jerks, swings dog, hanging toy, arm extended, twirls, twirls, twirls. Dog spins, around around, faster, increasing anger, until, grunt: MAN releases grip on toy. Dog flies. Four legs flail. Panic. Toy in jaw. Careen towards glass pane. Flashes: exploding pigeon, black feathers, gray feathers, bursting air, unfettered shriek, desperate squawk, animal sensing closeness, annihilation, body, preparing, sudden, final, contortion. Rushing through MAN's hea—

Suddenly, the thought hits him like it's nothing.

The dog's bark doesn't bother me.

His eyes shoot open and he lifts his head off the back of the cracked seat, where yellow foam pokes out between sharp gaps in the faux teal leather. A flow of unrecognizable liquids, some unplanned, break-in-case-of-emergency hormonal elixir, shoots from his chest into his stomach.

The dog's bark doesn't bother me.

The dog's bark doesn't bother him?

Because if the dog's bark doesn't bother him...

Has he merely been conditioned to believe the rest?

What have I done?

He immediately recoils at the nothingness of the thought, its immense roteness, total emptiness. He dizzies at his own lack of imagination, the inability to summon either profundity or clarity, his failure to organize into even a loose outline the jumbled noises pinging like lasers from one side of his skull to the other. Once upon a time he'd had all that, he felt, a certain richness which accompanied his memories, but he couldn't remember exactly what or when that'd been, and so much hollow time had elapsed in the meantime that he was filled right then, hyperaware of the molecules separating him from the firmness of his ripped blue bus seat, with a previously unimagined hollowness. He wants to cry—it might even elicit some sympathy from the rest of the bus, he thinks, though who knows with a crowd like this—but he can't. Dry, thin streams trickle down his face; the chaotic paths of imagined tears running down his cheeks burn.

Cut to WOMAN, sprawled out on the living room couch, reading. Nightfall approaches through the same large window in the background. The dark yard is empty. She flips the page. Cut to a close-up of her eyes, quickly scanning through words. Suddenly they stop in place and dart to the right, as if noticing something. Cut back to a wide shot of the couch amidst the room. WOMAN's eyes are frozen to the side. She sits up, turns her head to scan. The room is empty. She slides back into her reclined position on the couch, folding the book over her chest. She stares at the ceiling. Cut back to the close-up of her eyes. Her eyelids begin fluttering, growing heavier as she dozes off. They fall shut. The camera lingers on this close-up for several seconds. Cut to black.

Then again,

what right do I have to cry?

After all, it's not like it was so bad, what he'd done. Nothing at the level of a crime, certainly (although—no, no, it wasn't,

it wasn't, I made sure of i—YES, I'm positive. Not a trace. Nothing. Gloves, mask. No breaking, no entering. Well, yes. Entering. But. She'd given me the key. She'd given me—)

or even anything which might be pinned against him definitively by any legitimate source of authority. He'd let some people down, for sure. Broken some eggs to make an omelet, etc. That much he knew. But he'd very intentionally operated in a kind of gray area firmly on the side of admissibility, in a legalistic sense, but which nonetheless feels dubious for some reason he can't quite pin down. The fact of the word *motive*

's repeated appearance, burrowed somewhere deep within his eye sockets, looms.

Motive

How much of himself had he spent—thrashing nights, stinging follicles (if you can't trust ancestry.com with your biology, he'd reasoned, well, we may as well pack the whole thing in), intimate familiarity with terms like "Minnesota Multiphasic Personality Inventory"—attempting to unpack the word?

He'd been practicing the conversation in his head for months,

not that it'll ever play out, of course. Not that what I did was wrong.

The one about why.

Officer: And what, exactly, led to your decision to—

I: Well, officer, how far back would you like to go?

O: Excuse me?

I: How far back would you like to take things?

O: As far as you want.

I: As far as I want?

O: Yes.

I: Are you sure?

O: Sorry?

I: What route, exactly, would you like me to take?

O: I'm not following.

I: The long version or the short version?

O: I want to hear your version of ev—

I: Ah, he wants to hear my version of events!

O: Yes.

I: Well, Officer… Officer… Officer… Brady. Yes. Brady. I'm glad to hear it. Because I'm going to have to take it back, way back, to really get this thing sorted out. And I'd imagine you'll want a well-rounded understanding of my situation, no? Right. Sorely lacking that nowadays, huh? Roundedness. Sweeping curves! Confucius to Spinoza, Plato to Keynes! Overspecialization in the contemporary world! I'm here for the old-fashioned L.A. The Liberal Arts, Brady. Raaaaange ove—

O: Sir?

I: Libations of the mind, all they are to you. Never mind that the backbone of society, the spine of you, intellectually of course but also physically, the physical structures you walk on, all shaped by the impish whims of a handful of men, a few dozen, maybe—

O: I disagree fundamentally with that analysis of history, sir.

I: Come again?

O: You mistake the movers and shakers. You ignore the butchers, bakers, and candlestick makers. The ones pushing from the bottom up.

I: What's gotten into you, Bra—bottom up? Bottom up? Because, what? Your kids are in school right now reading the tomes of Earl the Exterminator and Leslie the Librarian? No. They're reading about Alexander and Caesar, Churchill and Napoleon—

O: Because the textbooks assigned in schools are the great arbiter of a society's will.

I: You understand my point.

O: I do. Which is why I'm all the more vociferous in my rebuttal.

I: Vociferous. Excellent, Brady. Excellent.

O: You don't think your overemphasis on the bourgeois in your analysis, sir, is in itself an indication of a certain…a certain…well, sir, I hate to push the allegation into such treacherous territory—

I: Go on, Brady.

O: A certain victim complex? If you will.

I: A victim? Me? Here? Sitting in this room, across from you, locked and loaded with a taser, a pistol, God knows what el—

O: Well, that's the funny thing, really. It appears in your determination to prove the subordinate status of the masses—butchers, bakers, Leslie, Earl— you yourself have (unintentionally, I'll charitably add, not to say ironically) grossly overrepresented the roles of the very men you proclaim the children's books of which you speak supposedly favor disproportionately. And, given the position you've just acknowledged you presently find yourself in, I'd say that leaves you in a real intellectual bind. A Catch-22 of sorts. Because say, as I anticipate you are about to, that it is not your wish for history to be taught this way. That you'd prefer it if my version, the bottom-up, power-to-the-people, resistance-of-the-masses type, were the modus operandi of the world writ large. Well, if in fact such a world came to pass (putting aside its utter lack of feasibility), you'd find yourself in an even tighter squeeze. Because, by your own logic, the baseline of this new world, its inner logic, deep foundations, would all be rooted in a context, historical and not, utterly transformed by this shift in perspective. So that suddenly there would be no Alexander, there would be no Caesar, no Napoleon, no Keynes. They'd be wiped from the history books, replaced by—and excuse my repeated deployment of our anonymous stock characters—butchers and bakers and Leslie and Earl. Who would then, the top of the deck suddenly (or not so suddenly, as such a counterfactual would surely require an extended period of historical uncoiling) clear, would undoubtedly find themselves subject to the very claims of historiographical overemphasis which you have just leveled against our current canon of prime movers. None of which, of course, presents as big of a problem for you, personally, as the most self-evident implication of your so-called utopia.

I: Self-evident?

O: Correct. Self-evident. The fact that, in such a universe, with all your previous Gods rushed off the stage, part and parcel, the deep understandings you've come to about history, the world, your place in it—they'd all evaporate along with your false idols. The stock you'd placed in their significance, faultily or not (and by now you know where I stand on that question) means their disappearance would lead instantaneously to a cratering of meaning, a torching of self-identity, a nadir of esteem, total confusion, a complete blank slate. Meaning, well—you wouldn't be you. And that's when your problems really begin, you see: when the trouble shifts from epistemological to ontological. From a murky and distant it to an icy clear, juggedly immediate me. When you realize the lines you'd been drawing between yourself and the world aren't just permeable but nonexistent. A complete veneer, a total ruse. Every question you've ever asked is about you. We all face such a revelatory moment. The switch flips, the spotlight flashes bright in your eyes. What do you do?

I: And—you?

O: *Well, quite frankly, sir, it's not my job to provide an answer. I'll admit that my younger self, the one preoccupied with the very jar of pickles you presently find yourself drowning in, burned an inordinate amount of energy attempting to solve a series of quandaries not unlike the one you've just presented to me. But after years of toil, countless lost nights of sleep, untold explorations through the most myopic of cerebral channels, I had the strangest realization.*

I: Which was?

O: That I don't have to.

I: Sorry?

O: I'm a local police officer. A glorified traffic cop. I don't have to think about it.

I: And I'm a—

O: Yeah, yeah. I know what you are.

I: We're practically the same.

O: No.

I: What?

O: No. We're not.

I: Why not?

O: Because I've already had the realization. I can't go back.

I: You've no idea what I've done. Do you?

O: You broke no laws. You said it yourself. I am bound by the contours of the law. It's better this way.

I: I don't think you understand. I want you to arrest me.

O: I know.

I: And?

O: As I said. Stop looking around. Face yourself.

The bus sighs to a stop under a slanted, concrete overhang. He shakes his head slowly, succumbing to the urge to prove his disappointment in himself to some amorphous onlooker. Eyes open but a vague otherworldliness attached to the images flashing by. Degeneration after degeneration, bursts of intelligible jargon superseded by an incessant tendency to stray from the point. He longs for both worlds equally and simultaneously; his nose strains for the scent of the redbuds blooming out the window while he lusts over the fluorescent interrogation room,

naughty plumes of cigarette smoke twirling towards the ceiling in defiance of gravity.

Why could he never meet anyone

like me?

If he could just find one person—

one person!

—who could both hold the flower up to his face and

see through my skull, understand the genius of my imagined worlds

(the ones too pure to write down), he could get off this godforsaken bus, emanating must like an evaporating sponge, and nestle up to her, forever. He could

let go.

Shit

he thinks.

Slipping again. Slipping, slipping,

slipping—

Wide shot of the living room from the opposite angle, facing the big window. Nighttime. WOMAN is passed out on the couch, curled up on her side, book splayed on the ground. Total silence. Slight movement in the background. The camera remains still. A dark, round FIGURE—the shape of a masked head—emerges above a railing blocking an ascending staircase visible behind the sleeping WOMAN. The head rises at a slow, careful speed, so precisely that it appears to be gliding up the stairs, maintaining a smooth, diagonal trajectory. WOMAN remains fast asleep.

For a long time, this is how he experiences the world: internal equivocation, cloudy hallucination, fuzzy pontification, elaborate, arcane, automatic arguments with himself influenced vaguely by the shadows of the strangers who happen to be surrounding him at any given time. These dialogues, he knows, change nothing about the course of his life or the world around him, yet, for the same mindless reason they occur in the first place, he is unwilling, unable (within his warped reality—

and that's the problem, isn't it, that I understand it to be warped

—the words are synonymous) to break free from them. His experience is devoid of physicality, impervious to particles, immune always, as if by the work of an invisible shield, to cool breezes, to the tingling brush of spiky autumn leaves tickling the hairs on his nose. All around him pounding jackhammers slam into cement foundations, men ascend electric lifts to dig rusted clamps into beams pressed together by bolts the size of fibulas. He knows, intuitively, that this is why the buildings in front of him rise so quickly. But he can't grasp the actuality of it all. One day a lot is occupied by one thing, and some time later a skyscraper with a spire occasionally lost in the clouds appears there instead. Process eludes him. He observes people, objects, and systems, but they simply float by, swept by a meek current he can't catch, a dribbling river parting always in the exact spot where he stands.

FIGURE continues emerging up stairs. Total silence. FIGURE has characteristics of a tall, lanky man, but his identity remains unclear as he's covered head-to-toe in black: shoes, pants, turtleneck, gloves, ski mask. In his right hand he limply holds a pair of scissors. He emerges from the staircase, moving slowly, methodically, and silently towards the back of the couch where WOMAN sleeps. He reaches the couch, stops, and looks down. Cut to a position below the front of the couch, with WOMAN blurred and out of focus in the foreground. FIGURE stares down at her. Both bodies are motionless. The screen cuts to black.

This, on its own, would be disillusioning enough. The real trouble, though, is that even though he can't touch it, he still senses, acutely, as one might be moved to tears by listening to a speech he cannot hear, all of it passing by, right in front of his face. He longs for touch, lusts over the imagined satisfaction of the weight exchange triggered by settling into a cold, concave bus seat. His complacency is self-imposed only insofar as it is regulated by an automatic set of levers operating somewhere inside himself; he doesn't know where, exactly, they are, much less how to operate them, but he is aware, at least generally, of their existence. Thus his perpetual state is accompanied always not only by numbness but by the tortuous tension between a lethargic reality and a vague, imagined vibrancy which he swears,

I swear,

he'd known once. His efforts to break into the world of movers and shakers amount always to attempts to accelerate into full-blown sprints using feet incapable of gripping the earth.

The screen flashes abruptly to a close-up of a white wireless internet router, its various lights flickering red, and a cord jutting out from its side. This image is accompanied by a silence-breaking sound; in the background, the bathroom sink is running. As in the flossing scene, the sound is emphasized. The shot is still. The router is on the dusty floor, and in the background, out of focus, the scene in the living room is visible; there's the vague outline of WOMAN in the same position on the couch, the kitchen where she'd been washing dishes, the staircase behind her. Flickering router lights, sound of running water, for several seconds. Abruptly, there's movement from the side of the frame. A hand covered in a black glove enters the shot, scissors protruded, and quickly, violently, severs the cord connecting the router. The dim house-lights briefly flicker, and the flashing router lights go dark. The sink continues to run.

By the time he attempts to break free from this self-imposed jail, he has become so conditioned to process experience through his particular subatomic prism that he loses the capacity to distinguish between the physical and the mental, between what can be touched and the vacuum his fingers slip through as they graze the empty atmosphere, gliding by a mason jar illuminated by a flickering firefly slamming, over and over, into the thin, curved glass surrounding it.

Wide shot of the room. Masked FIGURE glides back towards the couch, scissors in hand. He moves evenly, effortlessly, silently. He arrives at the same spot behind the couch, standing directly over WOMAN. The scissors dangle in an open position from his right hand.

This conditioning has blunted not only his capacity to separate the profound from the mundane but robbed him almost entirely of the ability to decipher reality from fiction, lived from imagined. He confuses billowing cumulus clouds for the shapes he sees when he closes his eyes, mistakes the slight sink of a mattress with the stomach-dropping dread of rolling off the bed, and conflates her voice with the anonymous one which echoes in his dreams. Which is why it's so obvious, preordained, that now that he'd actually done it, summoned the courage to break the barrier, place both feet on the ground, join the cacophonous garble, the scintillating pinch, the crushing gravity of the physical worl—

Cut to a low angle in front of the couch. Both characters in focus: WOMAN in the foreground, sleeping, and FIGURE looming behind her. FIGURE's shoulders rise and fall: a big inhale and exhale. Slowly, he lifts the open scissors towards his chest, blades facing the camera, before abruptly swinging the object directly towards—

The dog barks again.

Fucking dog.

Swot Core:
On Becca Rothfeld's *All Things Are Too Small* and the Agonies of the Liberal Critic

Udith Dematagoda

In *Contingency, Irony, and Solidarity* (1989), Richard Rorty perceptively noted that Vladimir Nabokov hated Sigmund Freud

> in the same obsessive and intense way that Heidegger resented Nietzsche. In both cases, it was resentment of the precursor who may already have written all one's best lines.

At first glance, Becca Rothfeld's essay collection *All Things Are Too Small* (2024) seems free of this specific type of resentment, partly because she seems oblivious to the possibility that anyone else could have already written her lines. She's unaware, too, that the grand philosophical and aesthetic problems she haphazardly attempts to address in her work were written about more substantively (and elegantly) by Rorty himself in 1989, and again almost a decade ago by the literary scholar Amanda Anderson in *Bleak Liberalism* (2016). Yet despite her grand ambitions, perhaps these aren't the type of ideas she wishes to be in dialogue with. Indeed, as is evident in this book and elsewhere, the actual obsessive targets of Rothfeld's antipathy (other writers of similar background and temperament) reveal a great deal about her real motivations.

We may defer the more erudite matter of intellectual pedigree for the moment, since it isn't entirely clear whether this is a serious philosophical or critical work on a par with Rorty or Anderson, whether it's intended to be pop criticism (most of its material relates to TV and cinema), or indeed personal memoir. The most memorable feature is an uncomfortable degree of abject detail concerning the author's personal life and trauma. This "trauma" is, of course, very much in keeping with the current moment. Nevertheless, one would expect a book with such grandiloquent stated ambitions to resist the urge to deploy what is by now a shopworn tactic, namely, the use of emotional deflection (*qua* blackmail) to obscure a certain flimsiness of ideas. If we can attempt to summon the declared purpose of this amorphous, rambling, and over-long collection (*All Things, All the Time* may have been a more apt title), it is that Rothfeld is a believer in Liberalism's promise of public equality, whilst also in favour of a hierarchy of artistic talent and aesthetic quality characterised by her own peculiar interpretations of "maximalism" and "excess." Clearly, she also believes that she ought to be somewhere near the top of any such hierarchy. Needless to say: this belief is somewhat unwarranted.

Indeed, what is given out to be a hierarchy is rather a trite and unthinking insistence upon those bourgeois stratifications of "good taste" most succinctly described by Pierre Bourdieu in *La Distinction* (1979). As a result, even the most potentially transgressive episodes of this work have the quality of safely recuperated opinions that bear the imprimatur of middling *bien-pensant* thinking. These opinions, conveyed in a diligently inane and prolix style, struggle to set themselves apart from the author's too-easy targets of lowbrow (and middlebrow) cultural output. The book, in general, is laden with almost textbook examples of the type of pseudo-profundity Nabokov had in mind with his own definition of *Poshlost* (to wit: "Corny trash, vulgar clichés, Philistinism in all its phases, imitations of imitations, bogus profundities, crude, moronic and dishonest pseudo-literature," etc.). I'm practising a lot of restraint by not enumerating them in detail (I didn't want to be too "mean"), because it's always merciful to resist the urge to be "maximalist" when engaging in stringent criticism.

Nonetheless, *Elle se croit...*, as it were. Arrogance and weaponized vulnerability are a confusing and disarming combination of traits in a writer, not least because they render any attempt at serious criticism socially perilous. When a writer intentionally intertwines the substance of their dubious intellectual project with the uncomfortable and awkward minutiae of their personal life, they have, in my view, rather cynically created a *cordon sanitaire* around the former, one which threatens to erase the distinction between criticism as an intellectual activity, and criticism as mere personal invective.

The above strategy seems to have been gleaned from two strands of historically feminist discourse that have until recent years enjoyed an uneasy co-existence. The first is *écriture féminine's* insistence upon personal, often abject, female vulnerability as a legitimate means of symbolic expression. The second is the now thoroughly compromised persuasion of 2000s *Lean In* corporate feminist culture; the one which enjoined women to adopt preening, somewhat aggressive personas—to become unapologetic in their self-belief to advance their career interests in a male-dominated world. In retrospect, this latter ideology was exemplified by a popular tote bag and t-shirt slogan from the 2010s: "Carry yourself with the confidence of a mediocre White Man." The most powerful rejoinder to a world dominated by "mediocre white men" would have been one populated by self-evidently brilliant women. However, the actual strategy seems to have been to simply replace men with women, not realizing that the central issue may have been mediocrity itself. The ignoble failure of Kamala Harris—not a white man, but emphatically a mediocrity—should sound a forewarning of the waning powers of this persuasion of liberal identitarian corporatist feminism (a "vibe" shift, as it were). In many ways, Rothfeld's book and her writerly persona occupy a similar psychic territory. But what exactly is it?

Rorty was one of the most respected figures of post-war American philosophy. Yet *Contingency, Irony and Solidarity* was a departure, notable for its rejection of the moribund technocratic preoccupations of the analytic philosophical tradition within which he had previously worked. In this book, Rorty makes a bold—if ultimately quixotic—attempt to interrogate the very category of "truth" against the inescapable contingency of historical reality and its myriad forms of symbolic representation. The book was part of a larger project to demonstrate how "continental" and "analytic" philosophy were complementary rather than antagonistic. To his credit, Rorty understood that no matter how rigorous an analytical philosophical account of aesthetics was, in the end, it would leave the majority of readers indifferent since the writing was invariably boring.

Philosophy, if it is to be compelling as philosophy and not merely as material for the exchange of professional shibboleths, ought to aspire to the quality of poetry. Even the most tortured and insane of analytic philosophers, Ludwig Wittgenstein, could scarcely approach the aphoristic and essayistic quality of popular philosophers such as Nietzsche or Sartre, who, in rejecting the stilted technical lexicon of professional philosophy, will perhaps remain the most popular in modern history. Rorty's motivations were noble and admirable. Like many men of his generation, he was raised as a fervent believer in the American political theology of "liberal justice" and convinced of its inherent virtue. When reading this later work, however, we're confronted with a palpable determination not to succumb to despair and disillusionment, perhaps instilled by an awareness of the sordid realities of American imperialism, made most apparent to him in later life by the criminal follies of the Iraq War.

Rorty focused not on the bureaucratic abstractions of liberal thought ordinarily associated with those who he called the "public philosophers," such as Jürgen Habermas and John Rawls (whom Rothfeld is fond of)—but on the private use of "irony" deployed to unite humanity in a universal opposition to all forms of "cruelty." Towards the end of his life, Rorty believed rather pessimistically that the liberal progressive cause needed "a specifically secularist form of moral fervor, one which centers around citizens' respect for one another rather than on the nation's relation to God." His 1989 work was a prelude to this later disillusionment and a clear attempt at a fundamental account of the humanistic roots of the liberal *Ideological Aesthetic* and its moral underpinnings. In this specific endeavour, he was—in my opinion—somewhat successful. However, if the overall purpose was to be understood as an attempt to reinvigorate Liberalism as a political and aesthetic project, it was an unequivocal failure. The moral fervour he sought to champion simply does not exist in the form he imagined.

The consequences of this failure were readily, if not always explicitly, acknowledged within the American academy, which is characteristically partisan in its overt identification with a liberal centrist ideological tendency, despite its efforts to cast itself as "radical" in its pursuit of various identitarian subjectivities. The tenured American academic, and aspirants to that condition, are fervent liberals in deed if not always in word. This is evident in their practical modes of living which I've had occasion to witness first-hand; purposefully isolated, insulated and sometimes deliberately segregated from the material concerns and lifeworld of their fellow citizens, whom they generally hold in contempt for their backwardness and vulgarity. This isolation, entirely self-inflicted, inevitably comes with a myriad of doubts. First among them is a concern about what American liberalism signifies within the aesthetic sphere aside from the ruthlessly enforced monopoly on the realm of "taste," which is invariably hollow and unsatisfactory.

This was the object of Amanda Anderson's 2016 study, informed by an "acute awareness of the challenges and often bleak prospects" that confronted liberalism. Anderson does well to illuminate the intellectual impasses faced by the liberal project and acknowledges just how imperilled it is in the present. Anderson is candid about the associations many have with liberalism as an aesthetic and critical doctrine:

> we associate what we call the experience of the aesthetic with the values of incompleteness, complexity, difficulty, excess, aporia. These values shift in emphasis, and they can be mapped in relation to familiar oppositions: beautiful/ sublime, liberal/radical, human/inhuman. What is salient for the purposes of this book, however, is that even in their tamer liberal humanist non-sublime forms, these aesthetic values clash with the investments of normative liberal philosophy, democratic proceduralism, and the mundane aspects of participatory and state politics... Against these, the aesthetic temperament values the implicit, the tacit, paradox, and a rich opacity.

This statement hints at the main problem associated with the desirability of a liberal *ideological aesthetic* to artists and writers, a point which Anderson later makes explicit:

> It must be conceded that thinkers within the liberal tradition have contributed to the situation in which liberalism is seen to have a deficient if not antagonistic relation to aesthetic values and modes. Indeed, to the extent that self-identified liberal thinkers have implicitly or explicitly

taken up the question of liberalism's relation to the aesthetic, there has been a tendency to refuse or at least evade the development of a liberal aesthetics that encompasses the forms and practices of political liberalism itself.

As Anderson correctly asserts, and as Rorty was loathe to admit, liberalism as an ideological tendency is generally inimical to the aesthetic ambitions of any worthwhile artist. Yet this liberal anxiety about art and aesthetics—such as it exists—derives not from liberalism's marginalization but from its status as the dominant ideology, as the centre, the uncontested default position of social relations for the *bien pensant* (surely an ironic designation). But as Rorty well understood—and as Anderson explicitly attempted to defend against—liberal centrism as an ideology is not generally conducive to artistic genius, which invariably exists on the peripheries or indeed at the extremes.

The Nazi political philosopher Carl Schmitt's *Political Romanticism* (1919) was an acerbic attack on the values of bourgeois liberal democracy as it existed in his time, a thesis which depicted the disappearance of God and its replacement with a certain "species" of occasionalism as the roots of the aesthetic Romanticism. According to this occasionalism, which according to him underpins the liberal bourgeois political project, the individual assumes the role once occupied by God as the arbiter of truth, justice, beauty, good, and evil,

> only in a bourgeois world that isolates the individual in the domain of the intellectual, makes the individual its own point of reference, and imposes upon it the entire burden that otherwise was hierarchically distributed among different functions in a social order. In this society, it is left to the private individual to be his own priest. But not only that. Because of the central significance and consistency of the religious, it is also left to him to be his own poet, his own philosopher, his own king, and his own master builder in the cathedral of his personality.

This gives some account of political liberalism's potential origins, but Schmitt would ultimately argue that being a "Political Romantic" is in no way tethered to liberal political positions, but rather to aesthetic ones. It was in this observation—made long before his own opportunistic involvement in Fascist politics—that Schmitt theorised how the basic premises of liberal subjectivity are the most fertile ground, and logical waypoint, for the development of Fascism, which was (and is) simultaneously an ideological and an aesthetic phenomenon. However, it was on the left and right of the liberal centre that the figure of the political romantic flourished. On the left, we have the origins of the radical positions inspired by the fiery aesthetic Romanticism of Byron, Shelley, Coleridge, Wordsworth, Hölderlin et al.—which would, in turn, inspire political revolutionary figures such as the Decembrist Kondraty Ryleev among others, and movements that would later assume the exhortations toward "divine" violence. On the right, we have an equally substantial aesthetic tradition that lays claim to perennial truths about human nature and boasts work that was the product of faith, constancy and devotion. This conservative tendency was, to my mind, best summed up by the Russian émigré poet and critic Vladislav Khodasevich, a beloved contemporary of Nabokov (who was, after all, a conservative writer), as those who aspire to be keepers of the flame instead of fire extinguishers.

In marked contrast, the "reasonable" and "moderate" expectations of liberal ideologues do not tend to be inspiring to artists of merit and ambition, who invariably operate on a level of elevated intensity which, in all times and all places, is vehemently opposed to the staid solidity and complacent mediocrity of the bourgeois establishment, and its paltry mercantile calculations. What Rothfeld fails to understand is that aesthetic excess is not the realm of Liberalism. It never has been and it never can be. It is possible that liberal criticism can admire such excess, as it often has, but only at a safe remove, only in spectacular ways, or (as in her case) once it has been safely recuperated. In my view, the primary reason—never acknowledged by those who tend to describe themselves as "liberals"—is that the nature of Liberalism's self-belief, its self-designation, is manifestly disingenuous.

The fundamental principle of Liberalism is not fairness, or equity—nor justice. It is hypocrisy. We are here firmly on the ground of the Platonic Noble Lie, of myths propagated by a self-appointed elite to curb the masses' propensity for violence. The vaunted ideals of

Liberalism are merely sleights of hand that obscure true, invariably economic and rapacious, motivations. This is borne out by the fact that many of the most morally bankrupt atrocities over the past 200 years, right up to the present, have resulted from liberal political and economic calculations; from chattel slavery, colonialism, the dropping of atomic bombs on civilian populations, non-intervention in conditions of famine, the privileging of corporate power over human lives at every level—to the current impunity and material support offered by the "West" to a supposedly "Modern Liberal Democratic" ethno-state conducting a revenge campaign of mass murder on women and children, in defiance of all "liberal" legal norms and standards. Liberalism has no compelling aesthetic because it is ultimately deceitful and calculating, and underhanded dishonesty never makes for sublime art.

The worldview one can infer from Rothfeld's work is very much adjacent to the previously described tendency of the American academic, even if we allow that it exists on the distinctly middle-brow plane of popular journalistic criticism, and is thus aimed at that mythical (near-extinct) figure of the "General Reader." The overarching argument of Rothfeld's book is a truism: that compelling art derives not from superficial and facile "goodness," but rather from ambivalence. It's an argument that does not need to be made. Nonetheless, she attempts to make this argument more tendentious (in favour of liberalism) than is necessary. Ultimately, this requires a Sisyphean intellectual task clearly beyond her capabilities and knowledge, as it was beyond the far more substantial intellects of both Rorty and Anderson. The task is to champion a specifically liberal, and worthwhile, aesthetic mode that ought to be the blueprint for the future. She approaches it in a rather odd way, by hinting at this amorphous account of a liberal aesthetics of "excess," in contradistinction to both Rorty and Anderson who grudgingly accepted that it was humanist moderation and subtle irony where the minor art of liberalism might hope to prevail.

The material she considers is also odd. For Rothfeld, there is much to disdain about the infantile tastes and predilections of ordinary people—and these provide most of the easy targets for critique. Of course this disdain is often couched in the diffident pose of the American liberal "Socialist" of 2016 vintage, who in retrospect was a reconfiguration of the Fabian socialist patrician of the 19th and early 20th Centuries. This figure already seems to be a relic of a bygone era—one brilliantly captured in all of his tedious, flabby, and frivolous glory in Matthew Gasda's forthcoming novel *The Sleepers*—but there is a certain value in Rothfeld's explicit statement of that turgid ideological project:

> My book does not argue against egalitarianism in every incarnation, much less against redistributive efforts in the economic domain. Rather, it is an argument in favor of a careful interrogation of the proper limits of the egalitarian project – limits that keep attitudes proper to the political sphere from crossing over into the *emotional and aesthetic realms*. Economic justice would surely improve the quality of art, for all of the reasons Marx and Schiller identified. Talented people would be less frequently stymied and have more opportunities to hone their gifts. Aesthetic culture as a whole would improve if audiences had the time and the *education* to cultivate their tastes. But if democratizing politics would go some way toward improving culture, the reverse does not hold: democratizing culture has gone no way towards improving politics. It has only left consequential inequalities intact, while depriving us of the extravagance that is our human due. (Emphasis added)

Rothfeld is, throughout this book and elsewhere, obsessed with "dues" and "entitlements." Aside from amply demonstrating the rather peculiar intellectual dilettantism and tortuously "correct" texture of Rothfeld's expository writing style, the above excerpt is revealing in many other ways. We cannot fail to notice a distinct whiff of patronizing complacency in this statement, which becomes an almost overpowering stench as the book progresses. "Education," as Ideological State Apparatus *par excellence*, has often been the clarion call of the upstart bourgeois intellectual, the aspirant to "elite" spaces who understands that the acquisition of qualifications, accolades and credentials is the only sure-fire way to ascend to a realm populated by one's social betters, where one may be permitted to lead lives of "cultivated" taste. They still believe fervently in the efficacy of education as a means of social advancement, and, as a result, they abhor those they deem too stupid to make use of such cynical stratagems.

Educational credentials are another of Rothfeld's peculiar fixations in this book; those with whom she sympathises are honoured with their "due"—such as "Oxford Professor Amia Srinavasian," and others with whom she doesn't derisively become only "Freelance polemicist Louise Perry." This is an easy observation. There is another, perhaps somewhat more alembicated, to be found in the facile conflation of the "emotional" and "aesthetic" realms.

I've written previously about the most important, and often forgotten, facet of Jean Baudrillard's famed essay *Simulacra and Simulation*, namely his description of the "liberating claim of subjecthood," which we can understand as a form of bribery customarily accepted by those who aspire to move within the PMC media and intellectual class. This "bribe" is, as I have observed, predicated upon the acceptance of a certain "hyperreality" *vis-à-vis* news narratives and assumptions. Baudrillard outlined well the recompense offered to the compliant bourgeois journalist/artist/critic in accepting a certain compromise:

> constituting ourselves as subjects, of liberating ourselves, of liberating ourselves, expressing ourselves at whatever cost, of voting, producing, deciding, speaking, participating, playing the game—a form of blackmail an ultimatum just as serious as the other, even more serious today. To a system whose argument is oppression and repression, the strategic resistance is the liberating claim of subjecthood.

The veracity of Baudrillard's claim of subjecthood seems to be expressive of an unacknowledged tension which I believe is in evidence through literary and art history from the late 19th century to the present—and is, I contend, a corollary to Jonathan Crary's thesis in *Suspensions of Perception* (1999). The emergence and evolution of a literary subjectivity according to the requisite temporal and attentive demands of Capitalist production, has been experienced as a liberation for certain classes—whilst simultaneously a foreclosure of the potential of revolutionary action. It is, in my view, most evident within the realm of "liberal" cultural production, and Rothfeld's collection is in this sense a very interesting document of its coordinates. Aside from the name-dropping of liberal thinkers and critics such as John Rawls and Lionel Trilling, there are other subtle hints such as the casual allusion to a "Judeo-Christian" tradition (an imperial ideology rather than a theological concept). These shibboleths signal her allegiance to the regime of Liberal subjecthood.

Slightly more difficult to discern is how the aggressively emotional affect of these essays signals the above intent in a far more sophisticated manner than any mere overt lip service. I briefly had a girlfriend who was obsessed in the early 2010s with reading the often sordid and salacious personal essays on websites such as Thought Catalogue and XOJane. I sometimes read them myself on her prompting, but could never quite shake the sense that they were obscene humiliation rituals that made the reader complicit in a form of gratuitous voyeurism. That specific genre of over-sharing personal essay is best considered alongside the American discourse on "therapy" insomuch as they both serve the function of a liberal, secular confessional. However, the point of this culture of over-sharing is not to unburden oneself to better serve the cause of collective or universal salvation, but rather to comply with the liberal injunction to serve only oneself and one's needs first and foremost. Perhaps the origins of this tendency are found within the *ecriture feminine* tradition we previously touched upon, yet clearly it has gone far beyond these initial confines. I sense that Rothfeld's collection is more akin to this "literary" tradition than it is to the probing examinations of liberal aesthetics by the likes of Rorty, Trilling, Anderson, et al.

In *A Theory of Literary Production* (1966), Pierre Machery offered an important insight into the essential difference between the writer and the critic:

What can be said of the work can never be confused with what the work itself is saying, because two distinct kinds of discourse which differ in both form and content are being superimposed. Thus, between the writer and the critic, an irreducible difference must be posited right from the beginning: not the difference between two points of view on the same object, but the exclusion separating two forms of discourse that have nothing in common.

> To be clear, I have absolutely no claims upon the title of "critic," or any title whatsoever. I have a day job as a scholar, but only by virtue of being over-educated and having acquired an accent, a certain convincing pose, and some measure of knowledge about literary history. It is for me nothing more than a job, and any notion of career advancement has

always been a matter of supreme indifference. That Becca Rothfeld insists on the title of "literary critic" is interesting beyond it being a quaint and anachronistic description, and the transparent strategy to position herself as the inheritor of Susan Sontag or Elizabeth Hardwick.

Such an insistence occurs at a time which seems stubbornly intent on bridging Machery's "irreducible difference"—an era dominated by the ubiquitous journalist/novelist/critic, where little distinguishes those formerly separate categories. In this regard, perhaps Rothfeld's critical writing may be motivated by a need to produce the conditions conducive to the appreciation of her version of an ideal novelist, which in all likelihood will turn out to be her future self. Perhaps she seeks, to paraphrase Roman Jakobsen, to transform herself from a Professor of Zoology into an elephant. Indeed, this disparate collection begins to cohere when we see Rothfeld less as a literary critic and more as a peculiarly contemporary type of "influencer"—a "maximalist" cultural factotum; a content creator, who aspires to be all things to everyone, and thus inspiring no one.

While we patiently await her auto-fictional debut, it's worth noting that, although Rothfeld is oblivious to the scholarly antecedents of her critical project, she is not without her obsessive targets of envy and resentment. Her choices are revealing much in the manner of Nabokov's reflexive abhorrence of Freud. Her most prominent *bête noires*, in a rather disappointing betrayal of the Sisterhood™, seem to be two more successful women writers, Sally Rooney and Lauren Oyler. This hapless, seemingly territorial, antipathy suggests some interesting points of commonality. All of them seem to have attended elite universities, but more interestingly all of them were involved in the high school debate club circuit. In the case of Sally Rooney, she got her break after a literary agent read her essay about being the "top competitive debater in Europe"; Lauren Oyler spoke in an interview about her use of the debate club as a way to fluff her CV for Ivy League applications. Rothfeld herself writes a particularly uncomfortable essay about her experience of the debating world, which paints it as a completely pointless exercise in hollowed-out bureaucratic thinking, appealing only to the pathologically maladroit. But much like Oyler and Rooney, the practice of debate ultimately comes across less as an odd eccentric passion and more as simply another box to tick while climbing the greasy pole of liberal subjecthood.

I must admit to a certain temperamental aversion to this type of "try-hard" thinking, particularly within the artistic, literary and intellectual spheres. I seem to have a visceral disdain for conspicuous effort, much preferring those who convey the eternally admirable principle of *Sprezzatura* made famous by Baldesar Castiglione's *The Book of the Courtier* (1528):

> I have found quite a universal rule which in this matter seems to me valid above all other, and in all human affairs whether in word or deed: and that is to avoid affectation in every way possible... to practice in all things a certain sprezzatura, so as to conceal all art and make whatever is done or said appear to be without effort and almost without any thought about it.

I speak also as someone whose own undergraduate university career consisted of assiduously calculating the minimum number of seminars one could attend to still get an attendance grade, and somehow still missing those—when not turning up extremely hungover or on a massive comedown (often both). I've always been instinctively suspicious of overt effort and striving. This was something that was the domain of what me, and my idiot mates, customarily referred to as "Swots," an excellent and percussive British English word which has no worthy competitor. Although impenitent toffs such as the anthropomorphic Toby Jug (and former Prime Minister) Boris Johnson have disparagingly used the term "Girly Swot," the term has no distinguishable gender: a Swot can be male or female. I'm unsure what the American equivalent may be—"hall monitor" seems the most descriptive analogue, but doesn't quite get there. *If you liked school, you'll love work* is the operational mentality. Whatever else they may be; their debate-club pedigree, their conspicuous and obsessive fixation with their perceived status, their box-ticking approach to writing, criticism, intellectual, emotional, and libidinal activity should alert us to the fact that Becca Rothfeld, Lauren Oyler, and Sally Rooney may indeed be some variation of the Swot archetype. I suspect that their prominence within the current moment speaks to the fact that the media and political class also seem, these days, to be mostly composed of people like them. Most are spiritual technocrats who seem incapable of transcending their petty infantile grievances, often in embarrassingly candid ways apparent in their writing. They are seemingly incapable of getting over a view of the world as High School cafeteria.

The Swot has a talent for diligence rather than intelligence or creativity, and there are few writers or artists of genius that belong to such a category. The type of genius worthy of respect is more often than not completely at odds with the structures and hierarchies that the Swot thrives within. In writing, the Swot requires the comforting bureaucratic logic of the editorial relationship—which has replaced that of the teacher, their erstwhile saviour and benefactor. Critics in the same vein that Rothfeld desperately wishes to be considered alongside—Susan Sontag, for example—were very far from being Swots, because they took pains not to appear so obviously and meticulously calculating, and were in possession of a belligerent and unconventional intelligence that sometimes made them personally abrasive and unpleasant. I'm unsure whether the same can be said of Rothfeld, who I assume to be pleasant enough—if her "approachable" public persona is any indication. She is in general a competent writer but very far from a stylist in the manner of Sontag, and far too easily swayed by the prosaic instincts of the litigious grammarian. In short, she is the type of writer who may talk loudly and fondly about the finer points of the Oxford comma, or similar inanities, to convince others of their commitment to the "craft." But there is a distinction between literariness and studied bookishness. The former speaks to certain intangible qualities, and the latter merely signifies an individual who is overfamiliar with a popular taxonomy of "types," and performs accordingly.

The zombie-like persistence of contemporary letters and publishing in the past decade seems to be aided by the fact there is no "literary" reading public to speak of anymore. It is no oversight that the tools of real-time analysis of sales, such as Nielsen Bookscan, exist behind prohibitively expensive membership fees, jealously guarded and beyond the means of ordinary people. I happen to have access to this service, and I therefore know how many copies this book—and others such as Lauren Oyler's recent offering—have sold. Needless to say, the numbers do not warrant the type of confected attention and dutiful reviews lavished on them across the media. This attention is merely evidence of a specific type of top-down solidarity, a quid pro quo—not necessarily one of "class" (or not only), but of those who perhaps find common cause with their fellow Swots. Many of the readers of these books—and I suspect the vast majority of Rothfeld's fans—are writers in waiting, motivated by the same delusions of acceptance, validation, escape from precarity, and *ressentiment*. They are aspirants to the sham world order of the Swot—one which attempts to force respect and intellectual integrity by bureaucratic fiat.

Rothfeld is, then—undoubtedly much to her chagrin—less a celebrity literary critic of the Sontag type than she is an Influencer in the current mode, and in the current moment. In this sense—perhaps as a small comfort—she does sit near the top of a certain hierarchy. This is a tendency which at its more vulgar echelons has given us things such as "Booktok" and "Dark Academia"... that is to say, confused accretions, by-products of a thoroughly compromised *hyperreality*, underpinned by the minor liberal *ideological aesthetic* and bound by its bribe of subjecthood. Something, in short, that merely approximates the appearance of intellectual activity rather than practices it. We are here very much on the familiar path of parasocial relations and "Mimetic Desire." But, as I have mentioned several before, such theories are incomplete if we fail to acknowledge that mimetic desire is in the current iteration of culture a negative dialectic, an *interpassive* relation where subjects delegate to others not only to perform actions but also to feel and suffer all manner of negative effects and emotions, on their behalf. Thus Rothfeld's successes, failures, thoughts, feelings, suffering, and "trauma" now belong not only to her—but also to her readers. In this sense, she is ultimately deserving of sympathy. She seems to have outsourced the task of self-actualization to the Bourgeois Big Other in various ways: through the confessional of the mandatory personal essay style, through the bribe of liberal subjecthood and the hypocritical acceptance of the political status-quo, through an unwavering belief in the regime of "education," credentials, institutional accolades, and achievements that are supposed to ameliorate what is clearly a meagre sense of self. But anonymous approbation, and cold professional regard, are poor substitutes for self-respect.

A Pound of Flesh:
On *A Year on Earth With Mr. Hell* by Young Kim

Jessica Baldanza

Young Kim's *A Year on Earth With Mr. Hell* recounts the ten-odd months around 2016 the author spent in an erotic, largely epistolary affair with the aged punk icon and writer Richard Hell (Richard Meyers) while she traveled, shopped, and grieved her late boyfriend of over a decade, the English punk impresario and fashion designer, Malcolm McLaren. Hell is "not happy" about the book, Kim admitted during a 2020 appearance on Brett Easton Ellis's eponymous podcast—indeed, he has publicly denounced it as revenge porn, but she exempts herself from obligation to Hell's privacy under the same rubric she employs in excusing his myriad transgressions: in art the ends always justify the means.

After attracting a cult audience of cosmopolitan writers including Ellis, Edmund White, and music journalist Greil Marcus following its 2020 publication by the NYC-based Ubu Gallery's press, *A Year on Earth* was republished by Fashionbeast editions in 2022. Having drawn attention for its notorious love interest and salacious subject matter, the memoir's success is due in large part to its surprising novelistic quality, drawn from the hero's journey Kim chronicles as both narrator and protagonist. She sets the stage for her affair by describing the inborn sense of aesthetic ambition that saw her transcend an isolated and illness-ridden childhood and adolescence in Long Island, NY, making it to Yale and eventually Paris, where she met McLaren at a party for his ex-partner, the designer Vivienne Westwood. Kim, then 26 and a virgin, commenced a romantic relationship with McLaren (25 or so years older), with whom she lived between Paris and NYC until his death from Mesothelioma in 2010, at which point it was revealed he had named her his sole heir and executor of his estate, infamously excluding his only son. It is in the latter role that she meets Hell, soliciting him to present an award in McLaren's honor.

While narrating her first clandestine meeting with Hell, Kim explains that she experiences life "as [she] would experience a movie," complete with long shots, close-ups, and a soundtrack. Those early, lonely years spent in suburban, immigrant obscurity (her family emigrated to Long Island from Korea when she was a year old) apparently ensured that she, in the tradition of Emma Bovary, would mediate experience through the media she consumes. (Here one thinks, too, of Michel Houellebecq's axiom that those who love life do not read, nor do they go to the movies.) Without irony or self-consciousness, Kim makes reference to Maupassant and Faulkner when sparring wits with Hell, but it is Ian Fleming's James Bond novels; *Animal House*; Woody Allen, Clive Donner, and Peter Sellers's comedy *What's New Pussycat?*; and, above all, that epic tale of female tenacity, Margaret Mitchell's *Gone With the Wind*, that have shaped her worldview. Kim's literary and filmic influences are most palpable in her gender essentialism, which is so profound as to render her union with Hell nearly inter-species: "Men are wonderfully bestial," she writes, in sustained awe and fascination with Hell's "leonine" features, his "broad nose," and "lewdly luscious" lips.

Men are, according to Kim, "visual," men don't say what they mean, a man would never send a woman a long message unless he wanted something from her, men don't react right away, men pick up where they leave off (whereas women take time to be reacquainted), and so on. While she claims to take sexual equality for granted, her summoning of traditional notions of men's and women's roles as distinct yet complementary (woman as the neck to man's head, etc.) is significant to the extent that in a largely desexed, nominally egalitarian culture of the sort she and Hell exist in, such views can no longer be taken as a given, and so suggest literary influence and a penchant for bygone eras. By the end of the book, once the affair has inevitably shriveled to nothing, Kim soothes herself with the thought of writing, concluding, "with all the hardship I've lived through, I've become a man."

Kim does not seek to understand Hell (whose decidedly masculine and somewhat vulgar otherness is a constant source of amusement and bemusement for her), but to win his attention, to engage with him to the extent that she can keep her fun and her fantasy alive. Accordingly, she reminds us (and herself, it seems) regularly of what an "artist" and "poet" Hell is. Hell shares in Kim's fanciful tendencies where they coincide with his erotic ones, but is distracted and weighed down by various pedestrian troubles. The pregnant anticipation, built up through their long-distance correspondence and released in periodic meetings in chic NYC restaurants and hotel rooms, is not infrequently diminished for Kim by Hell making reference to one wearying fact of his personal life or another. Kim, who in youth took pains to "blot out" any ugliness that entered her periphery, and who has manifested an adult life most could only dream of, does not appreciate these encroachments of the real, particularly as she is painfully aware of the elusiveness of the "epistolary," "romantic," and (ironically phrased) "real world" expiring along with McLaren and Hell's generation. Reminders of Hell's "rapidly deteriorating" body deflate her, as do the legal troubles relating to his recent divorce, and the hollow remorse he feels over betraying his new girlfriend. This last qualm Kim dismisses as a matter of his American puritanism, which she considers a naive and possibly self-indulgent quality in a man who described himself as a "slut" in his own memoir.

Beyond Hell's "dark chthonic sexual force," Kim finds a surprisingly hapless, befuddled individual, a sexagenarian still "in trouble with too many women," still pawing around in the dark of his own consciousness with a hard on. "I haven't been the kind of son she expected," he says rather depressingly in reference to his mother, yet another woman he is disappointing (whereas Kim, ever the pragmatist, "doesn't care a whit about [her] grandmother"). She is patient with Hell, albeit fatigued by his MSNBC-addled emotionality with regard to Trump, his philistinic scandalization at her prodding mention of Ayn Rand. She regularly claims an unwavering affection for him even while coolly observing his contradictions, his failed promises to her, the weight he could stand to lose around his middle. She excuses his interpersonal transgressions in light of his being an artist—a class she sees as entitled, even *obliged*, to narcissism, as "any artist of any worth was one." What wears her patience are, rather, his intermittent appeals to monogamy and the concomitant guilt and shame he carries around like St. Augustine before the conversion, even while sending her obscene text messages of eggplant and peach emojis. He starts to bore her.

Nevertheless, Kim is reluctant to let Hell go, to lose. Whereas McLaren's purported neediness complemented her "need to be needed," Hell stubbornly resists Kim's endeavors to assimilate him, refusing to become an official character in her narrative. He begrudgingly accepts Kim's legal counsel, but rejects her medical advice and her offer of organic, free-range eggs (her solution to the dubious nutritional merit of his supermarket ones). He loses interest or resolve often enough that Kim, with all the manic mischief of Melanie Daniels in Hitchcock's *The Birds*, must regularly resort to her arsenal of erotic emails and elaborately conceived, innuendo-filled gifts including a French, perfumed handkerchief emblazoned with the word "Dirty," and a suggestive "diptych" of the Eiffel Tower. The procuring, preparing, giving and receiving of gifts precede and/or follow every one of her sexual encounters with Hell, so that for each paragraph documenting his sexual mastery, there are three more dedicated to her shopping for, wrapping, and perfuming presents. Kim's penultimate gift to Hell is a specially procured artisanal knife from Austria, with the word "Penetrate" engraved along the blade, and "Richard Coeur de Lion" along the handle. She selects a Hamlet quote card that reads *This above all, to thine own self be true*, and writes inside, *CAPITULATE to the indomitable!!!* (the indomitable being his base nature, and herself), kisses a lipstick print into it and stabs the card through with the knife (eliciting images of Mia Farrow's infamous 1992 Valentine to Woody Allen after discovering his affair with her daughter), before sending it all wrapped in tissue and mailed in a Hermès box. "*He would appreciate its beauty whether he wanted to or not,*" she thinks about Hell receiving her latest gift, "*He had taste and was susceptible to beauty.*"

Hell is skeptical of fashion, but loves beauty; it is a value they share. Beauty was Kim's north star in her isolated adolescence, art her permanent recourse to the problem of life. This fact is inscribed in every one of her sumptuous descriptions of meals, sex, travel, couture, and the book object itself, whose design is an homage to Olympia Press, the Paris-based publishing house that produced first editions of erotic and banned books including Nabokov's *Lolita* and the anonymously penned *The Story of O*. Kim's book, discrete in size but bold in design, is a small work of art and auteurism after a decade of largely anonymous collaboration with McLaren.

Their affair took place six or so years after McLaren's death, when Kim, aged 40-something, had presumably survived the worst of her loss, and Hell, 68, had divorced his wife of twenty years (ostensibly due to his infidelities) and entered into a new relationship with another woman. To accommodate Kim's extensive traveling and Hell's stated dislike of speaking over the phone (a selective luddism consistent with his outsider persona), their relationship manifested much like the romance in critic Joanna Walsh's 2018 "novel in essays" *Break.up*: through email, text message, letters, and postcards. It was after their first encounter in a hotel room that Hell asked Kim to write him something "dirty," describing what they'd done from her perspective. Happy to acquiesce, she cites her fulfillment of his request as the catalyst for her secretly writing about the affair, having found delight (and perhaps a sense of control) in this novel outlet.

At some point during the affair, while Kim recorded and narrativized her relationship with Hell, unbeknownst to him, he became her muse, and she became an arriviste-cum-artist (and thus, in her own view, woman-cum-man). Via this inversion of the expected dynamic with an older male artist, Kim poetically fulfilled the trajectory started by her late partner decades before, who found a muse for his magnum opus, the Sex Pistols, in Hell's spiky hair, torn shirts and nihilistic ethos. "The muse is particular to the person," she writes. "What one artist may be inspired by, others might be left scratching their heads about. The personal relationship can be positive or destructive—and often is—but it ultimately leads to creation, which is all that matters."' In extending her logic to herself, Kim is only asking that Hell understand her, first and foremost, as the fellow artist she's become during their affair, and that he, denuded by its publishing, nevertheless judge her memoir as an artwork. If Hell's pride is a casualty of this pure endeavour, Kim insists, not entirely convincingly, that it is just that, casual—a coincidence.

The epigraph to the 2022 edition of *A Year on Earth* features four quotations, one from Lucius Apuleius' *The Most Pleasant and Delectable Tale of the Marriage of Cupid and Psyche*, one from a song written by McLaren, one from a song of Hell's, and one spoken by James Bond in Ian Fleming's novel *Goldfinger*: "Some Love is fire, some love is rust. But the finest, cleanest love is lust." It's an appealing premise, flattering to both Hell and Kim, but the pretense of a spontaneous, pure attraction doesn't quite apply here; excepting her romantic bent, Kim is no Emma, no little *bovariste* shopping and fucking in vain, unable to meaningfully escape her bourgeois, provincial surroundings. *Kim made it to Paris*, she spanned the distance literally and metaphysically, thus proving herself to be a protagonist more worthy of Stendhal than Flaubert—the Julien Sorel of legacy fashion media. Aside from implicitly carrying on McLaren's project, Kim's admitted "ruthless practicality" casts doubt on her carrying out a relationship that isn't also, in a word, practical. She's a believer in apprenticeship, and Hell is, she mentions multiple times, only the third man she'd slept with. "I wasn't going to let him get away like that," she writes early on, "I enjoyed the affair, but I also wanted my pound of flesh."

The final scene of *A Year on Earth With Mr. Hell* describes Hell abruptly abandoning a naked, post-coital Kim in a hotel room amidst his latest crisis of conscience. The reader's implicit sympathy for her is at this point tempered by a sense of the narrator's unreliability, her penchant for the cinematic, her Tom Ripley-esque will to power. Kim reinvented herself upon entrance to Yale, and again in her relationship with McLaren. Whether calculated at the time of her initial carnal attraction to Hell or not, Kim has, much to Hell's discomfort, successfully leveraged their relationship into the next arc of her life—*Kim the author*.

In the aforementioned podcast, Ellis wonders aloud whether he would have been so engrossed in Kim's book if her love interest had not been the famous Hell, before dismissing the question as immaterial, as Kim did sleep with Hell, and she wrote about it in clean, stylish prose with startlingly intimate detail. She got her pound of flesh, and if the addition of "No.1" to the cover of the second printed edition is suggestive of a sequel, she'll have another.

www.ingramcontent.com/pod-product-compliance
Lightning Source LLC
Chambersburg PA
CBHW011650010726
47496CB00012B/3019